THE RENEGADE

Joel Meadows

NEW HARBOR PRESS

RAPID CITY, SD

Meadows/New Harbor Press
1601 Mt Rushmore Rd, Ste 3288
Rapid City, SD 57701
www.newharborpress.com

Ordering Information:
Quantity sales. Special discounts are available on quantity purchases by corporations, associations, and others. For details, contact the "Special Sales Department" at the address above.

The Renegade / Joel Meadow. -- 1st ed.

Our light can swallow up your darkness; but your darkness cannot now infect our light.

—C.S. Lewis

"**C**ITIZENS OF REAVELLA, PLEASE have your identification out and ready to show to the security detail," the announcement said as it blasted out over the city. The world was full of skyscrapers and towers as cars hovered in the air with three moons shining in the night sky. The creatures of this world were just as different as the city they inhabited. Some resembled animals from our world but others were unique, for example, some resembled a fox but had the head of a lion. "A Protector has been spotted in the area. Please have your identification ready. The punishment for not complying is treason against the dark king," the announcement ordered as creatures resembling ravens dressed in dark black armor walked down the sidewalk searching the crowd. As a blockade started to form at the end of this neon street figures started to walk through the crowd but they were dressed in armor and had a helmet covering their face. They walked through the crowd passing creatures as everyone pulled out an identification card.

"Suits working perfectly, no security alerts are going out," a male voice said through a speaker inside the helmet.

"You doubted?" The figure asked with a muffled voice, making it unrecognizable.

"Only slightly," the male voice answered.

"Now you tell me," the stranger replied.

"Turn here," the voice said through the speaker just as the figure walked up to the wall of troopers. The stranger turned down a small alleyway with a small light stand on the other end. They walked down the hall and rounded the corner to see another small figure waiting in the shadows.

"Who's that?" The small mouselike creature asked as the armored stranger walked underneath the light post. The stranger reached up and took off their helmet. She was a teenage wolf girl with bright white fur, blond hair, and bright blue eyes. "Are you?" The mouse started to ask.

"Were you expecting someone else?" She answered with a smile knowing the rest of the question.

"What are you doing here?" The mouse asked.

"When we heard what was happening, we had to come to help you," the girl answered.

"You risked your life for me?" The mouse asked in amazement.

"Just part of the job description," she answered as she reached into her pocket. "Here," the girl said holding out a small computer chip. "Take this override key and head into Market Seventy-Five. Scan this and an automated ship will get you out of the city," she explained as the mouse took the chip.

"Thank you," he said holding the device in his hand. Just as everything was calm lights shone brightly from behind them.

"Hey, you," a raven said shining his flashlight at the two.

"Go, I got this," she whispered looking at the mouse.

"Thank you," the mouse whispered one last time as it slid back into the shadows.

"Put your hands in the air," the dark trooper ordered. She started to put her hands in the air with the helmet still in her hand. Suddenly she put the helmet on and started running into the city. "Stop!" The trooper yelled as they started chasing after the figure. She ran out of the alleyway and into the streets as the officers pursued her. They grabbed their weapons and started to fire dark purple blasts at the figure. She ducked as she ran up to a fire escape ladder that led to the rooftops but it was at least two stories in the air. Just as the troopers thought they had the figure, she jumped up in the air and grabbed the ladder as if it were just a simple hop on the sidewalk. She grabbed the ladder at first with one hand, then with both hands as she started to climb up. "She's heading up to the rooftops, send air support," the raven ordered knowing who the stranger was just by that simple act. She climbed as fast as she could and she reached the top just in time to see a hovercraft coming over the rooftops.

"Hey, I'm going to need some help," she said into the mic in the helmet

"I'm on my way," the voice replied as the aircraft started to fly over the roofs. "Where do I find you?" He asked.

"Don't worry you'll know," she answered as she started running over the roofs of the city as more troopers opened fire, shooting up at the armored figure. "Just like any other night," she said as she ran.

The best, most beautiful, and most perfect way that we have of expressing a sweet concord of mind to each other is by music.

—Jonathan Edwards

THE SCHOOL BELL RANG out as the students ran out of the classrooms. Brant Wilson walked out of the room with his hands full of books as he walked down the hall. He walked by a large window on the second floor of the school to see the Golden Gate Bridge off in the distance. Brant was like any other student with his bright white skin, black hair, and brown eyes. He walked down the hall and up to his locker that stood at the corner next to another hall. Brant opened the door and started to put his things in his backpack when something came behind him and pushed his head to the back wall of the locker.

"Hey, loser," the voice said. Brant turned around to see the school bully with an evil grin on his face.

"Hello, Allen," Brant said as he turned back toward his locker.

"Where were you yesterday? Did you stay home afraid of the world?" Allen asked with a smirk.

"No, I was out on the bay having a wonderful time by myself. Any chance I get to not be with you is an opportunity I take," Brant answered grabbing his bag and closing the door to his locker. "Disappointed?" He asked back with a smirk.

"Yeah, I missed beating your face into the ground," Allen answered as Brant started to walk away.

"Believe me, the last thing I missed was smelling you," Brant replied with a grin as he walked away. Allen smashed the locker as hard as he could, creating a dent as Brant just walked away.

He walked around a corner to see a group of students hanging around and talking. "Hello," he said with a smile.

"Hey, reject," the girl closest to him said with a grin as Brant walked by. He didn't have many friends. Not because he didn't try, he tried as hard as he could but everyone saw him as this weird kid with a sarcastic sense of humor, but he never could make a connection with anyone. Brant tried but everyone always reminded him of why they never wanted to be with him. "You're an orphan who was abandoned, why would we want to hang out with a reject like you?" They would ask every time he would try to make a connection but he was used to it, if you can ever get used to something like that. He walked down the flight of stairs that led to the main entrance to the school. Brant reached his hand out and pushed the door open as he stepped out into the California light. Brant reached into his pocket and pulled out a set of EarPods, placed them in his ears, and hit the play button making *Letters to the President* by Hawk Nelson play through his ears. Brant bobbed his head as the music played.

"When we were younger, we used to sit on my porch and talk smack about girls and professional sports," Brant listened as he walked. *"There's a lot of things I wanted to say but never got a chance to find a way,"* he sang as he walked. Brant walked as the music played and he mouthed along to the lyrics as if no one was watching. Brant walked along the sidewalk passing apartment complex by complex as he sang along. *"And so I thought I write a letter to the president and have him pass it to the leaders of the Parliament, but for now I won't say nothing,"* he listened as he walked. Brant rounded a corner only a block from school as he made his way down the pathway. He walked up to a building not too far from the main sidewalk with a sign over its doors that read *San Fransisco Orphanage* and in smaller writing just underneath it, *reeding giving a second chance to those who need it.* Brant walked up and

opened the wooden doors and stepped inside the lobby of the orphanage he called home. The room was a light gray with windows on the back wall where a desk sat with two chairs in front of it. Brant started to walk up to a door right next to the desk as an old man sat behind the computer typing away.

"Brant," he said with a smile looking up from his computer just in time to see Brant before he opened the door.

"Hello, Mr. Sim," Brant said with a smile stopping before he left the room. Mr. Sim had been there for years and everyone knew who he was, and he always loved being with the kids, and even the young teenagers like Brant.

"How are you?" Mr. Sim asked. "It's been a couple of days since I've seen you."

"Alright, I guess," Brant answered making sure he gave Mr. Sim the respect he deserved.

"How's school?" He questioned with a smile.

"Okay," Brant answered truthfully.

"Glad to hear," Mr. Sim replied.

"See you later," Brant said as he started to open the door but was stopped.

"Brant," Mr. Sim said making him stop. "How come you don't hang out with the others?" He asked. "You have a good sense of humor, you're outgoing, and you have enough confidence to accomplish anything you put your mind to. What do you say?" Mr. Sim asked. Brant looked down at the floor contemplating the question, then he looked back at the old man.

"I appreciate the offer, Mr. Sim, but I'm doing just fine by myself," he answered to Mr. Sim's surprise.

"You sure?" He asked. "You can find a place where you're wanted."

"I'm not sure I'm wanted anywhere," he said as he walked through the door.

"You'd be surprised," Mr. Sim said as the door closed. Brant walked down the hall with doors on both sides leading to rooms. He walked up to a wooden door and opened it, walking into his room. It wasn't anything extravagant, but it had a small bed with a nightstand right next to it, a small TV, and a door on the right side of the room that led to a small bathroom and a small cabinet for his clothes just beside the bathroom. Brant walked in and dropped his backpack off by the nightstand and sat in bed pulling out a small bag of Doritos left over from his lunch that now acted as his dinner. Granted he could've joined everyone else and have a much bigger meal, but he didn't feel like socializing.

He got his dinner as he sat on his bed. He turned the TV on to local news. As Brant ate his dinner, he watched the news as they gave the weather and a news story that explained that a group of thieves robbed two museums in the span of twenty-four hours stealing ancient artifacts. Brant cleaned the crumbs off his bed and started getting ready for bed as the Golden Gate Bridge shone in the night. He changed into his pajamas and crawled into bed as the moon hung high in the sky.

"Another day come and gone," he said to himself as he lay in bed. "Maybe tomorrow will be different," Brant said as he started to dose off. "I probably shouldn't get my hopes up, but hey who doesn't love a guy with such a great sense of optimism," Brant said joking to himself as he fell asleep.

THE ALARM BLASTED AS the sun came through the shades. Brant reached over, turned off the alarm, and ran out of bed as fast as he could. He ran to his closet, grabbed jeans and a blue T-shirt, and headed to the bathroom. Brant got ready as fast as he could brushing his teeth, changed as fast as he could, and headed back out by his bed. As he walked through the living room Brant turned on the TV to the local news again and some music as the iconic guitar melody of *Meant to Live* by Switchfoot started just to have something playing in the background. Brant got this breakfast which was only a granola bar and sat down on his bed just as another news story about thieves robbing museums came on again.

"That's dumb," Brant said watching the TV. He finished eating and started to clean up when he pulled his phone out to see the time. "Whoa, I gotta go!" He said running behind. He slid his phone and EarPods back into his pocket and ran over to grab his backpack still by the nightstand and ran out the door. Brant ran down the hall and into the lobby where Mr. Sim was by his desk with two smaller kids.

"Have a good day, Brant," Mr. Sim said with a wave.

"Thanks, you too," Brant said turning around to face Mr. Sim as he walked toward the door.

"Hey, be careful out there, who knows where those robbers will pop up," he said as Brant stepped in front of the sliding doors.

"It's okay, I'm not a relic yet," he joked winking at the old man.

"Oh, that's good," Mr. Sim said with a chuckle.

"Have a good one," Brant said with a wave as he turned back around and headed back down the street as the morning sun shone down on the city.

4

BRANT STARTED WALKING DOWN the street as he made his way to school. He rounded the corner as the sun shone on the city. He walked around the block passing stores that were opening for the day. Just as Brant started to come to the end of the street with his school just around one more block, sirens started to blare. He stopped as the ear-piercing sound grew louder and louder. Suddenly a pickup truck with a group of men in ski masks sped around the bend with the police right behind them.

"Whoa!" Brant said taking a step back as they came up on the sidewalk for a moment making the truck bounce. Some of their loot started to fall out as Brant watched a small golden ball fall out.

"Hey, we lost it!" The first thief said in the back of the beat-up truck.

"Leave it!" The driver yelled back as they sped away. Brant took off his backpack as he walked up to the golden orb and picked it up just as the police sped by.

"Police," Brant said picking it up and turning back to the road. "They dropped—" he started but by that time they were gone. "This," Brant said standing alone on the sidewalk. He looked down at the artifact he picked up. It was a golden orb with a small metal ring around its center. "What is this?" He asked himself looking it over. Brant held it up looking at the small ring and turned it on both sides one clockwise and the other counterclockwise. "Huh," Brant said a little amazed that he figured that out as quickly as he did just by turning the two ends.

He looked down at the orb and pulled on both sides making it slide open like a kitchen drawer revealing a hidden compartment. As soon as he slid it open a bright blue orb fell out landing in front of Brant's feet. He looked down at the orb as it started to roll by itself around him. Brant watched as it sped faster and faster creating a small blue wall so he couldn't get out of the circle.

"Hey," he said as he started to take a step toward the wall realizing he was being blocked. Before he was able to take another step the ground opened underneath his feet and he fell through. "Whoa!" He yelled as he fell. As soon as Brant fell the blue light vanished along with Brant and the golden orb with it.

"A H!" BRANT YELLED AS he fell through. He looked around to see stars and planets around him as he sped into the unknown. He looked in the direction he was flying to see an outline made by stars. Brant thought he was just flying aimlessly but it looked like he followed a path whether he wanted to or not. "Whoa!" He yelled again as he started moving upward to see a hectagon-looking door. "Wait, wait, wait," Brant said moving his arms and trying to slow down but he wasn't making any progress. Brant started moving faster and faster up. He shot through the octagon archway and flew up high in the air. "Whoa, whoa, whoa!" he closed his eyes ready to hit the pavement but he never did. Brant opened his eyes to see a golden sphere around him making him float. He looked around at the sphere at a loss for words. Suddenly, the sphere vanished and Brant fell to the ground head-first just as the golden orb rolled to a stop next to Brant. He lay on the ground for a moment with his eyes closed when a bright yellow light spiraled from the pavement ground as it hurled itself toward Brant till it touched his hands and feet; but, since his eyes were shut, he didn't see the strange anomaly. "Ow," he said rubbing his head and opening his eyes as he looked down at the street. Brant got on one knee and started to look up, but when he looked up, he was met with a small sheep dressed in a red dress. "Ah!" He yelled jumping back and landing on his backside.

"Ah!" The sheep yelled as she ran the other way. Brant got to his feet as fast as he could, watching the sheep run away. He looked around at his surroundings to see a city, but it wasn't like any city he'd seen before. Brant looked around at the massive buildings touching the sky and the cars that hovered on the roads just beside him. He took a step back bumping into someone.

"Oh, sorry," the voice said as Brant turned around. He turned around to see a tiger dressed in a suit. "Whoa!" The tiger said as their eyes met.

"Ah!" Brant yelled as he took a couple of steps back into the street. He looked around to see the pathway on both sides of the street full of anthropomorphic animals. "This isn't happening," Brant said to himself as he looked at the street full of animals glaring back at him. He looked around at everyone watching him. Thirty red shirts, ten white, and five blue. "How, did I know that?" Brant thought to himself. He turned around just in time to see a car hovering over the road. "Whoa!" Brant said lying on the ground as fast as he could. He looked up to see the hover car pass over him, then he stood back up to see the sidewalk crowded with even more creatures. "Thirty different types of spices," Brant thought to himself. "Wait, how am I doing that?" he asked himself. He wasn't even trying to count, he never had the chance to since he was turning his head every three seconds, but somehow, he still knew.

"What is that?" Someone asked as Brant just stood there not knowing what to do.

"Hey, you," a voice said from behind Brant. He turned around to see three creatures in dark armor walking toward him. They looked like ravens if they walked with two legs and had creepy armor all over their bodies. "Put your hands in the air," they ordered. Brant put both hands in the air as he watched the soldiers come closer and closer to him. They were in dark purple armor, equipped with a helmet in a skull-like shape, and had a blaster strapped to their waist. "Don't move," they ordered as Brant watched in terror. He looked around to see the street starting to empty. Just by looking at them, Brant could tell they didn't look friendly and the empty street just proved his thoughts. He looked around to try to find an escape. He looked to his left but it was a dead-end, but when he looked to his right, he saw a small alleyway. He didn't know where it led but it was away from the creeps with the helmets. Brant took off running as fast as he could down the unknown alleyway.

"Stop!" The trooper yelled as they pursued Brant, but the third soldier stopped when he kicked something on the ground. He looked down to see the orb as he picked it up off the street. He stared at the orb for a moment or two amazed about the object in his hand then back up in the direction of Brant as he ran into an unknown city.

BRANT TOOK OFF DOWN the small alleyway and out the other end to see a street with small restaurants and shops lining the sidewalk. He ran out into the street and looked behind him for a moment to see the two troopers chasing him. Brant ran down the middle street as the floating cars swerved out of his way while he sprinted as fast as he could. He ran down a main stretch of road that led to a small courtyard with skyscrapers towering overhead and a small fountain in its center. Brant stopped and looked around to see more anthropomorphic creatures stopping to stare at him.

"Stop!" He heard behind him. Brant turned around to see the masked creatures running up to him with their blasters drawn. Brant looked around to find a way out but it was hard to see through the crowd. He looked behind him to see a group of groundhogs walking toward him, and he got an idea. Brant took off running again jumping over the herd. He jumped farther and higher than he expected but Brant just kept running. "Stop!" The raven yelled again as they ran after Brant. He ran past a building that resembled a bank with a sleek white look to it but he kept running. Brant turned down another road with more shopping outlets and apartments but he didn't stop to look at the details. The troopers rounded the corner getting closer and closer to Brant as two bright-armored figures moved around on the roof a block ahead.

"Ready?" The first figure asked but their voice was muffled by the helmet.

"We're good to go," the second figure answered as they met up on the same side of the roof. "Hey, what's that?" He asked looking down at the street. The stranger looked down at the street to see Brant running.

"I don't know, but it's not our problem," the first figure responded.

"Come on, where's your sense of fun?" The first figure questioned back. "Besides, I want to dent their helmets," the second figure looked down at the street and took a deep breath.

"Okay," she responded. "I'll get him up here while you take care of the troopers."

"Got it," the first figured said, then he jumped over the side while the second stranger ran over to the fire escape filling the space between them and the building next door. She looked down to see the ladder raised off the ground. She waved her hand with the palm of her hand facing down toward the metal ladder, and as if she hit a switch, it slid down bouncing once or twice as it landed with a bang. Hearing the noise Brant looked down the small pathway to see the ladder. He turned as fast as he could and ran to the ladder and grabbed on with a death grip as he started to climb up to the first landing. He started to climb up as the troopers followed down the small pathway when they heard something land behind them. "Hey, freaks," He said making them turn around. As soon as their eyes met, they opened fire without saying a word. The figure ducked dodging the first blast while Brant ran up the stairs thinking the troopers were shooting at him.

Just as the second blast hurled toward the bright red-armored figure, he reached his hand out and stopped the dark purple laser in the air as bright yellow dust surrounded the blast. As fast as he could he waved his hand backhanded like he was hitting a tennis ball, and the blast shot back at the trooper even faster than before hitting the trooper in the chest causing him to fall on his back.

"That the best you got?" The stranger asked sarcastically. The trooper grunted as he continued to pull the trigger. The figure jumped over the first blast, landed, and held out his hand with the palm of his hand open. Suddenly, a bright yellow beam shot out flying through the air making a unique sound as it struck the trooper's helmet causing a dent as he fell to the ground. "Well, I'm satisfied," he said looking down at the dent. The figure jumped up to the first landing of the fire escape without even using the ladder Brant used as he ran up.

Brant ran to the top of the building, out of breath as he got closer to the roof. He stepped over the ledge and stopped to catch his breath. He bent over and placed his hand on his knees looking down at the metal roof underneath his feet. Brant took a deep breath after a deep breath as his brain tried to process what happened. He took another deep breath but the more he stood there the more he felt like someone was watching him. He looked up to see a figure dressed in bright orange armor with a helmet covering their face.

"Hey," she said looking at Brant. Brant took a step back toward the ledge when the figure from the street stepped up.

"Hey, how are you doing?" He asked patting Brant on the shoulder.

"Ah!" Brant yelled as he put his hand up, touching the figure. Brant closed his eyes as his hand landed on the figure's arm. Suddenly, Brant's hand lit up a bright yellow and sent the armored figure back hitting the ledge though Brant had no idea how he did it. The two figures looked at each other as Brant opened his eyes.

"How did you?" The second stranger asked herself as the first stranger got to his feet. Brant looked back and forth at the figures knowing they had him cornered.

"Who are you?" Brant asked. "What is this place?" He asked.

"It's okay," the second stranger reassured. She reached up and removed her helmet making a click as it came off. "Hi," she said with a smile. Brant's eyes got big for a moment looking over the creature in front of him. She looked like a fox with light orange fur with a touch of dark orange mixed in, even the hair between her ears was orange, and her bright yellow eyes looked different. Brant didn't know what made them unique, but there was something there. "It's okay," she reassured. Brant turned around at the other stranger just as he took his mask off to reveal a cheetah with yellow fur mixed with black dots, and just like the girl his eyes were different, or maybe it was something else, but Brant could feel something different, but at least they both looked the same age as him, so he had that going for him.

"Hey," he said with a grin.

"What is this place?" Brant asked again.

"It's okay," the girl reassured. "You're safe."

"Who are you? Why are you dressed like that? Why were they chasing me?" Brant said asking one question after another.

"Hey, hey, it's okay," the cheetah replied walking past Brant and standing next to the fox.

"Forgive me if I don't believe you," Brant said wishing he would get some answers.

"It's better than being chased by the masked creeps," the cheetah replied.

"What is this place?" Brant asked wishing he would get an answer.

"Don't worry, we can explain everything, but we can't stay here," the girl answered. "You're welcome to come with us."

"You sure that's a good idea?" The cheetah whispered to her.

"You saw what he did," she answered.

"You mean I felt what he did," he corrected. "But I don't even know what he is and I know you don't know either,"

"True, but if he did what we both think he did, he has to come with us," the fox explained. The cheetah looked at Brant for a moment then back at the fox.

"Fine, but you're going to be the one to explain it to her," he agreed.

"Fair enough," she said looking back at Brant. "You coming?" She asked. Brant looked at the creatures, then down at the street where he was being chased, and finally back at the two strangers.

"Okay," Brant answered. He didn't know if this was the right decision, but at least these creatures talked to him instead of chasing him immediately. On top of that, he felt at ease but he couldn't explain why, like a safe feeling in his chest and he didn't know why. "Why am I doing this?" He asked himself as he started following these creatures he just met.

BRANT FOLLOWED THE TWO strangers over the rooftops as he jumped over small gaps between structures and across pieces of plywood connecting others too far to jump. He followed the creatures up to a building taller than the others around with a ladder bolted to the side that led to the top.

"Hey, where are we going?" He asked looking up at the strangers.

"I'd tell you, but I'd have to kill you," the cheetah answered with a smirk making Brant second-guess the choice he made.

"Are you serious?" He asked.

"Don't worry, we're not going to kill you," the girl reassured.

"That was supposed to make me feel better?" Brant asked as he started to climb up the ladder. He climbed higher and higher till he reached the roof with a view of the city. Brant looked out to see towers as far as the eye could see with roads with multiple levels and a giant building in the shape of a sphere at the center of the city. He looked out over the cityscape as the creatures walked up next to Brant. "So, this isn't a dream? This is all real," he said, looking out over the night lights when the fox slammed her hand in the back of his head. "Ow!" He said rubbing his head.

"That hurt, right?" She asked.

"Yes," Brant answered in a why-did-you-do-that tone.

"Well, there's your answer," she replied as she walked over to the edge of the building.

"You know you're making every point that I should walk away right now for me," Brant said as the cheetah made his way to the edge of the building.

"Don't worry, you're in safe hands," the fox reassured. "Besides we're almost there."

"How reassuring," Brant said to himself as started to walk over to the edge of the roof. "Where is *there*, exactly?" He asked.

"Right there," the girl answered with a point. Brant followed her furry finger to see a rundown warehouse nestled between two skyscrapers.

"You're kidding?" Brant asked.

"Hey, you wanted to come," the cheetah replied.

"I keep telling myself that," he said back. "I don't know what's going on; I don't even know your names."

"Don't worry, once we get there, we'll answer some of your questions," she replied.

"Some?" Brant asked himself. This was getting ridiculous. He'd been chased only to come across these things, and they wouldn't even tell him their names; but, what choice did he have? He had no idea where he was or where to go, at least this seemed like a way to get some answers, and the way he felt he just wanted to know where he was at this point. "What's that building?" Brant asked looking at the massive silver sphere at the center of the city with red lines all around it.

"The capital," she answered after taking a deep breath. Brant nodded his head. He finally got an answer; granted he'll never have to remember that useless fact, but at least it was something. "So, maybe these things really will help me," he thought to himself as he walked up to the edge of the building. "I'll follow you."

"Of course, you will, you don't know where you're going," the cheetah replied. Brant couldn't tell if he was joking when he said things like that or if he was serious.

"Technically, he does. I just showed him," the girl replied.

"Yes, but he doesn't know how we're going to get there," he said in a tone that made it sound like he was serious but also a joke.

"Just follow us," the fox said as she jumped over the edge of the building and onto the fire escape.

"Did you know we would be going down?" The cheetah asked looking at Brant with one eyebrow raised.

"Wow, I'm shocked," he replied sarcastically as they started to move toward the street.

"Really?" The cheetah asked. "Your brain must be very fragile," he said as they walked down the metal-grated stairs.

AT THE CENTER OF the large city sat the capital. It was a large sphere with thin red lines that surrounded the silver circle lighting up the surrounding area a faint red. Inside the structure stood a great hall with a black carpet that led from the doors to the other end of the room where a small set of stairs stood, and a black throne sat on top overlooking the room. The doors slid open, and a guard stepped through. He looked around to see the room empty, so he started to make his way to the other end of the room. As he walked, he looked around the room. There were no windows just a light that hung from the ceiling and red lights on the floor that outlined the black carpet that led to the throne. Just as he stepped up to the small staircase, he looked up at the empty throne to see outlines of a battle on both sides of the arms that stretched to the floor. On the left side was one side of the conflict and on the right was another, and the images made it appear the side on the right was winning.

As the raven stood there alone in the room, a pair of doors opened suddenly on the wall behind the throne. He stood at attention as a figure walked through. She was a young girl, maybe fourteen or fifteen. Her skin was bright pink and partly see-through like a ghost. Her hair was dark pink, and she wore a short, dark pink dress that stopped at her knees and bounced off her bright ghost skin. She walked over and stood at the right side of the throne and crossed her arms. Before either one could say anything, a new figure walked through. He was older and taller than the girl with light gray skin, black hair that was up, and a robe, and his eyes were dark gray. The soldier got on one knee when he saw who he was in the presence of, as the dark figure sat down.

"My, lord," he said bowing his head.

"This better be good," he replied.

"It is," the raven reassured. "While I was patrolling Reavella I came across a creature," he started. "It was unlike anyone I'd ever seen. We went to search him, but he ran away and as he ran, he forgot this," he said holding up the orb. The girl uncrossed her arms in amazement as the dark figure straightened up. The king stood up and walked down the small flight of stairs and up to the soldier still on one knee. He bent down, took the golden orb from the raven's clawlike hand, and looked it over. He looked down at the center of the orb to see the line that divided both sides and tried to turn and open it; but, unlike Brant, it didn't open. "I think it's how he got here," the soldier added.

"Interesting," he said, still looking at the golden orb. "Who else knows about this?" He asked.

"No one," the trooper answered. "The men who were with me haven't returned."

"Good, we'll keep it between the two of us," the dark ruler said. The trooper looked around to see only the king and a girl in the room.

"Master Eclipse?" He questioned.

"Oh, don't worry, your discovery will be safe with us," Eclipse said as he held his hand out with the palm of his hand facing up. Suddenly a small black dagger formed in his hand like sand.

"Sir," the raven said but it was too late. With a wave, Eclipse threw the dagger, hitting the trooper in the chest as he fell to his back.

"Man, I wanted to do that," the ghost girl said walking down the small set of stairs and looking at the trooper lifeless on the ground.

"Don't worry, you'll have your chance, Darcy," Eclipse said in a rather soothing, deep voice as he looked down at the orb.

"I thought these were all destroyed?" Darcy asked pointing to the golden sphere.

"As did I," he answered. "But it would seem we have a new opportunity to try what we failed seven years ago."

"But what about this new guest we have?" She asked.

"Since he activated it to come here, I'm unable to open the orb," Eclipse started. "So, to achieve our goal I must have the key."

"I'll find him," Darcy said confidently as she turned toward the door but stopped.

"Be patient, my daughter," Eclipse said getting her to turn around. "We must play our cards right," he said, sitting down on his throne as he thought of what to do next. "Go to Market Seventy-Five. We know that they have some form of operation there, and I think it's time to find out where they go," he ordered. "Follow them and tell me where they stop."

"Father, I will not fail you," Darcy said with a bow as she turned to the door.

"And, Darcy," he said getting her attention one more time. "I want her alive," Darcy nodded her head, and she left the room while Eclipse sat on his throne staring at the orb in his hand, fighting back a smile as he sat on his dark throne.

B RANT FOLLOWED THE FOX and cheetah to the massive wooden doors that served as the entrance to the warehouse. Brant looked behind him to see the road empty. Wherever they were it wasn't a busy part of the city. Brant walked through the sliding wooden doors as the cheetah closed them behind him. He looked around at the interior of the rusted structure to see crates scattered all around and a new figure sitting on one of the crates near the center of the room.

"Hey, sis," he said hopping off and walking up to them. Brant watched as he walked over to the group. He was another fox-like creature with bright orange fur wearing a black T-shirt underneath a dark-drown bomber jacket and dark jeans. "How'd it go?" He asked with his slightly raspy voice.

"Okay," she answered. "But we have a new curve ball," she said as they took off their armor. Brant stepped to the side as they talked. He watched as the girl took off her armor to see the clothes underneath: a black T-shirt, dark green jacket, and black pants, and the cheetah had a black T-shirt with a graphic of what Brant assumed were letters, even though he didn't know what it meant, underneath a yellow jacket with dark blue jeans.

"What curve ball?" He asked, then he looked over at Brant who was standing next to a beam that ran up to the ceiling. "What is that?"

"I don't know," she whispered to her brother as she stepped next to him with the cheetah not far behind.

"And you brought him here?" He asked.

"I had to," she answered. "I think he has it," the girl answered.

"You're kidding," he replied not having to go into detail. He looked at his sister who nodded no as Brant walked up to the three.

"You know, if you're going to talk about me can you at least do it loud enough so I can hear," Brant said stepping up to everyone.

"It's not your business," the brother replied.

"I was the one being chased, you brought me here, so, yeah, it's my business," Brant said crossing his arms and standing his ground. Granted he didn't know why he was there but he wanted answers.

"His brain is incredibly fragile," the cheetah said in a tone that made Brant question whether it was a joke or not.

"I was being sarcastic," Brant said with a chuckle of disbelief.

"You have a name?" The girl asked seeing how things might turn rather quickly.

"Brant Wilson," he answered.

"That's a nice name," she replied. "I'm Kit," she said introducing herself.

"Nice to meet you," Brant said, relieved he at least was getting a name.

"And this is my brother, Alpha," Kit said introducing her brother.

"Nice to meet you," Brant said with a smile. "Finally, I'm getting somewhere," he thought to himself.

"The older brother," Alpha corrected.

"By five seconds," Kit said with a grin.

"Five seconds is still five seconds," Alpha replied with a smirk.

"So, wise," the cheetah said in his monotone voice.

"Oh, and this is Solar," Kit introduced.

"Nice to meet you," Brant said.

"Of course, it is," Solar said stating the obvious.

"Okay," Brant said looking at the ground for a second.

"You'll have to forgive him, he takes everything literally, and he has the same type of humor," Kit said defending him.

"At least he has a sense of humor," Brant said with a grin.

"Of course, I have a sense of humor, I've made a bunch of jokes but you haven't laughed at them," Solar said looking at Brant with a judgmental look.

"I thought you were serious," Brant said kind of embarrassed. He should've known but he was so out of his element he didn't know what to believe.

"It's okay, it took me a while to figure out if he was joking or being serious," Kit reassured.

"Sometimes I still can't tell," Alpha added.

"What do you mean? I'm so obvious," Solar said looking over at Alpha.

"No, you're not. You're supposed to change your voice to let everyone know you're kidding; you just keep everything the same tone," Alpha said.

"Why would I change my voice? I'm not ashamed of it," Solar said missing the point.

"Anyway," Kit said stopping the whole conversation. "Brant," she said getting his attention. "Feel a little bit better?" She asked.

"A little," he answered. He wanted to know more but he already felt at ease with these creatures, even with Alpha, and he didn't know why. "Now, mind telling me where I am?" He asked.

"Do you think you can wait a little longer," Kit answered. "Till we meet up with our leader."

"Wait, I thought you were the leader?" Brant asked looking at Alpha.

"You would think that wouldn't you," Alpha said looking at his sister.

"Don't give his ego any more ammo against us," Kit said rolling her eyes.

"Oh, I thought he was since we had to meet up with him," Brant said correcting himself.

"You're very perceptive," Alpha replied. "In truth we're—" he started but was cut off.

"Minions," Solar said.

"Minions?!" Alpha and Kit asked at the same time.

"We're freedom fighters," Kit corrected.

"Is that our job description?" Solar questioned back.

"Yes," she answered while Brant just stood there.

"Oh," Solar said looking at the ground for a moment, then up at Brant. "We're freedom fighters," he said like Brant didn't hear the conversation.

"I knew I shouldn't have come," Brant said starting to regret his decision.

"Don't worry, we can explain everything; but it would be easier if the whole team was together," Kit explained. Brant took a moment to think about it. He now got a few answers, just none of the important ones; but, at least, he was getting somewhere. Even through all of this, he felt at ease when he was around them, and he didn't know why. He kept trying to wrap his brain around it but was getting nowhere.

"I'll follow you," Brant said in amazement that he was still willing to keep going.

"Let's get going," Kit said with a smile walking back to the doors.

"I think you're going to regret that," Alpha added.

"I probably will, but at this point, my curiosity is getting the best of me," Brant said with a grin. Alpha looked at Brant and nodded with a grin on his face like he was impressed with how fast Brant came back at him as they all walked back out into the streets.

BRANT FOLLOWED THE GROUP down a neon street as they rounded a corner only a block from the warehouse. He rounded only one corner to see another street, but this was noticeably different. On both sides of the street were tents just like a fair with rags over the tops to provide shade or cover from the weather. Brant looked up to see a sign made of two pieces of plywood that read Market Seventy-Five spray-painted with its black ink smeared on the wood.

"Now, whatever you do, don't talk to anyone," Kit said as they walked underneath the market marquee. "If something happens, we can't help you."

"How reassuring," Brant replied as they walked down the center street. He looked around at the vendors of the market. Some had food the likes of which Brant had never seen before, while others had jewelry, and some had items that looked right of a sci-fi movie, but he didn't know what they were. Brant looked up to see lights hanging on a string that led from one tent to another lighting up the alleyway. He looked back down to see vendors and other shoppers look at Brant with a questionable glance as they walked. The clientele was just as sketchy as the market itself. "Why are we here?" He asked walking up to Kit.

"We have a hidden way out of the city tucked away here," she answered.

"Well, you couldn't have picked a worse place," Brant said looking around at the market.

"It's the last place they would come looking for us," Alpha added in his slightly raspy voice.

"Who's they?" He asked as they continued to walk.

"Later," Kit whispered as she walked. Brant just looked at her wishing he would get a straight answer, but he was going to have to wait some more. As they walked, people watched them pass but no one said a word. Either they were hiding themselves or they had more important matters to attend to than messing with them at the moment. They walked past a booth selling food that smelled terrible. Brant could only imagine what it tasted like if the smell was any indication. They stepped up to a brick wall, but all the bricks didn't match, almost as if someone pieced it together after the structure was built. "This is it," Kit said stopping with everyone just behind her.

"That's great, I was hoping to see this wall," Brant said sarcastically.

"It is a nice wall, isn't it?" Solar questioned back in the same monotone voice.

"I like to think of it as a work of art," Alpha added with a smirk.

"Do you want to stop and take a souvenir picture to mark the occasion?" Kit asked with a grin.

"That depends, do we have the time?" Alpha asked back with a smirk.

"Oh, shut up," Kit said to her brother as she turned back to the brick wall.

She reached her hand out with two fingers facing up to the sky. Suddenly, she snapped her wrist to the left with her fingers still in the air. As if Kit hit a switch, the wall moved as if it followed a command opening like a sliding door at Walmart.

Brant stood speechless to see the wall move, revealing a small set of stairs leading down to a platform.

"Whoa!" Brant said taken back by the moment.

"Pretty sweet, right?" Alpha asked seeing Brant was impressed.

"It was a nice wall," Brant answered and, to his surprise, he got them to chuckle, which was a first for them; but he was happy about it. "Maybe they aren't so bad," he thought to himself going back and forth not knowing if he should trust them completely or not, but that helped a little.

"We need to get out of here," Solar said, looking back to see if anyone was paying attention to them.

"Let's go," Kit said as she walked through the now-revealed doorway.

"After you," Brant said with a grin. He watched them walk in the hidden stairway and was about to follow when the hairs on the back of his head stood up. He looked down at the ground having the feeling they were being watched. Brant turned around but no one was there. He could hear the market packed just on the other end of the tent that was cooking food that smelled terrible, like cooking a lizard, but that was it. He looked to his left and then to his right, but no one was watching. Brant turned around and headed down the flight of hidden stairs just as the walls closed behind them, all while a figure watched from a roof just behind the group listening to every word, kneeling behind a chimney with her pink semitranslucent skin, watching the whole thing.

11

BRANT WALKED DOWN THE set of stairs as the wall closed behind him. He looked around to see the same brick pattern as he stepped farther and farther underground. He stepped onto the platform at the bottom of the stairs to see a station with a train parked standing only a few feet from a tunnel that led to who knows where. Brant looked at the train to see it not only as rusted as it could get, but some of the pieces looked like they might fall off at any moment.

"You're kidding," Brant said looking at the train.

"Not exactly what you expect when you hear *underground train*, huh?" Alpha asked as they walked up to the train.

"Well, we have something like this where I come from, but they look way better than this, and that's saying something," Brant answered as he looked up and down the rusted mode of transportation. "Do we have to get on this death trap?" Brant asked as they walked.

"Don't worry, it's perfectly safe," Solar reassured.

"Don't advertise perfectly," Kit added. Brant looked up at the head of the train and swallowed hard as he walked up to a small doorway that led inside the rusted train. "Is everything inside?" Kit asked.

"Good to go," Alpha answered as they stepped on board. Brant took a step up and inside the train to see a small room with seats on both sides of the car with tainted windows looking out over the station. They sat down in the beat-up, old seats so Brant did the same. He sat down making the seat creek like it was about to fall over.

Suddenly, the train jerked forward making Brant hit the back of his seat as the train started to creep. The train took off after it hesitated and sped into the tunnel. Brant looked out the window to see a concrete wall with the occasional light speeding past them as they traveled faster and faster. Brant started looking around the room feeling more at ease since the train didn't explode or fall off the track, though he still thought these might be a possibility.

"What do you think about him?" Alpha asked whispering to his sister.

"He seems all right," she whispered back.

"We thought the same thing about a lot of people only to have them stab us in the back," Alpha replied as the train continued to move.

"This one feels different," she said still whispering.

"I just hope you're right," he added.

"And if I'm not?" Kit asked.

"Then she'll never let you forget it," Alpha answered. Brant looked out the window as the train started moving upward till it shot out of the tunnel and into a field of trees as it leveled out still moving at a fast pace. He looked around to see trees as far as the eye could see. Some looked like trees where he was from, but others looked different with barks a dark orange color with dark yellow leaves. Brant looked out the other window across the aisleway to see more trees like they were in the middle of a forest. The train started to slow down, and a small building could be seen out of the corner of the window. The train pulled into a small wooden shack as it pulled to a stop inside.

"Looks like we're here," Kit said standing up.

"Of, course we're here, did you not know where you were going?" Solar asked as he stood up with Alpha not far behind.

"I was letting Brant know we were here," she replied.

"Then, why didn't you say so?" Solar added.

"She did," Alpha said as they stepped out. Brant smiled as he followed the group out. He stepped off the train and into a new station. It looked like a barn with dark wood planks as a roof and its structure was wide open with its supports on full display down to the beams that ran to the concrete floor holding everything up. He followed the group over to a pair of sliding doors on the other side of the makeshift station. Brant took a step out to see he was standing on top of a hill overlooking a small village with smaller houses every few feet.

"Wow," Brant said to himself not expecting to see a small village like this.

"Come on, we're almost there," Alpha said as the group started to walk. Brant followed the group as they started walking to the left while he looked around at everything. The village was built on the side of a hill with houses that stretched to the bottom of the hill where a small pond stood with more houses. Brant kept looking around to see a pathway that separated into three individual paths that led down to the pond creating a subdivision feel to it. He followed the group to the path farthest left and started walking down the hill passing small houses. They were about the size of a trailer or mobile home, but they looked like any other home you would find. Brant looked up to see three moons hanging in the night sky.

"Funny, I've been here how long and I just noticed that," he thought to himself. He looked back down to see the pond and the pathway that surrounded it with more homes just like the ones he was passing. Brant followed the group till they turned into one of the lots that was fourth from the bottom of the hill. "This is it?" He asked.

"This is it," Kit answered turning around and smiling at him for a moment. Brant followed the group underneath what looked like a carport with the front door up a step or two made of bricks. Brant looked at the house to see light-gray siding and a screen door before opening the bright white door just behind it. Alpha opened the door and stepped inside with Kit right behind him. Brant walked up to the door to see a welcome mat just below his feet.

"Please, wipe your feet," Solar said looking at Brant.

"I don't know if you're kidding or being serious, but I'll do it either way," he said with a chuckle. Brant wiped his feet, stepped up to the door, and stepped inside the small house, still not knowing why he was brought there, but he had a feeling he was about to find out.

12

BRANT TOOK A STEP inside the small home as Solar followed in behind and closed the door. He looked around to see a small living room with a couch and three chairs. Just a few feet away stood the kitchen with a few cabinets. Brant turned around for a second to see a small hallway that led to what looked like two bedrooms, and then he turned back around to see a small hallway just by the kitchen with two steps down that led to another bedroom.

"We're back," Kit said looking around. She listened but there wasn't any response.

"Hello?" Alpha asked listening for a response. They stood in the quiet living space when they heard a small cry from the bedroom by the kitchen followed by more grunts and sounds of pain.

"Wait here," Kit said as she started to walk toward the hallway. Brant watched her walk down the steps and into the bedroom closing the door behind her. She walked into the small room painted white with a black wall just behind the bed. Kit walked over to the bed where a teenage girl was sleeping. She lay on her stomach gritting her teeth as she slept wearing a turquoise tank top and black jeans. Kit quietly walked up as the sleeper continued to gasp like she was outrunning something in her dream. She stepped up to the bed and gently touched her arm. The girl opened her eyes as she grasped for air. She looked up to see Kit standing over her with a soft smile.

"Hey, Kit," she said looking up.

"Are you okay," Kit said as she sat up in bed. "You were breathing pretty hard."

"Yeah, that one felt different," she answered sitting at the edge of the bed. "It felt like something happened."

"Yeah," Kit started dreading what she had to tell her. "Something did happen," Kit said as she felt her leader just look at her with a look.

"What did you do?" She asked.

"It's a long story," Kit answered. "We brought it home for you to look over."

"You brought it home?" She asked.

"It's waiting for you in the living room," Kit explained standing up and walking over to the door. "And it's unlike anything I've ever seen," she said leaving the room.

"Oh, boy," the girl said standing up. She walked over to the door, grabbed a black jacket hanging on the back of the door, and walked out of the room. She walked up the two steps and headed toward the living room. Brant turned around when he heard the sound of footsteps while Alpha and Solar did the same. Kit walked into the room and turned around facing the hallway as a new figure stepped in. Brant raised his eyebrows for a moment looking over the creature that walked in. She looked like she was the same age as him, just like the others, but she looked like she was a wolf. She had light gray-and-white fur like a wolf with a small black nose. She had bright turquoise eyes and between her ears was bright blond hair that went down past her shoulders, and she wore a turquoise shirt underneath a black jacket with a blue-and-pink graphic on the right shoulder creating a pop of color.

"Are you a—?" She started to ask as their eyes met. "No way," she said stepping up to Brant. "It's a human," the stranger said looking over at Brant. "I mean you are a human, right? It's just you look so weird." She asked walking around Brant grabbing his arm and looking him over.

"Yeah," Brant answered as she walked behind him and grabbed his hair. "Whoa!" He said as she pulled his hair looking him over more.

"I've never met a human before," she said letting go of his hair and forcing his mouth open as she looked over his teeth.

"This is a first for me, too," Brant replied. She let go of his mouth and took a step back still looking him over from top to bottom. "Is it okay if the specimen asks who you are?" He asked.

"I'm Selene," she introduced. "Who are you?"

"This is Brant," Alpha answered before he had a chance to.

"Is there any good reason why you brought him here, or just because you felt like it?" Selene asked in a way that led Brant to think they'd done something like this before.

"We have reason to believe—" Kit started but stopped, biting her lip.

"Believe?" Selene questioned.

"We believe he has the light of Reavella," she finished.

"What?" Brant asked before anyone had a chance to say anything. "That's why you brought me here? You thought I had some kind of light power?" He asked with a chuckle.

"You used it on me," Solar answered.

"No, I didn't," Brant said not knowing what happened.

"I saw you do it," Kit added.

"So, let me get this straight," Selene started, stepping in the middle of the conversation. "My team thinks you have the forbidden light. So, they brought you back here, and now you're going to miraculously come in and save the day?" She asked sarcastically not believing any of it.

"Exactly," Solar said not knowing what sarcasm is.

"Yeah, you must seriously think I'm an idiot," Selene said dropping her ears back for a moment before raising them back up to their normal height.

"Thank you," Brant said with a grin. Selene just looked at him with a questionable look that took Brant a second or two to figure out. "Not the idiot part," he corrected.

"Well, we can find out right now," Alpha said looking at Selene.

"Go ahead," Selene said with a sigh still not believing. Alpha walked up to Brant and stood right in front of him as everyone watched.

"Hold your hands out," Alpha said looking at Brant. He looked around the room as everyone watched. Brant looked for a way out of the situation but, at this point, it looked like he would have to humor them.

"Okay," he said holding his hands out like he was carrying a box or showing a dog a large ball.

"Now, close your eyes," Alpha added. Brant just looked at him wishing he didn't have to do any of this, but he still didn't have any choice. He closed his eyes as the room stood silent. "Okay, I want you to picture in your mind a dark tunnel, and at the end of a tunnel is a light."

"Usually, people don't want to see that image," Brant said with a laugh.

"Just do it," Alpha replied. Brant pictured a tunnel with a light at the end of it with his eyes still closed. "Now, imagine that light in the darkness is coming from you," he said. Brant thought about it. He was standing in the tunnel and the light was all around him. He didn't know why he had that image, but it was the only one he could come up with at the moment. As he stood there, his hands were beginning to tingle when a bright yellow light suddenly rose from his hands, creating a unique noise as it traveled from one hand to the other.

"Ah!" Brant yelled, opening his eyes to see his hands lit up a bright yellow.

"Yes!" Alpha shouted as everyone looked at Brant with their mouths wide open. Selene looked at Brant's hands and then up at him with as much disbelief in her eyes as Brant did.

"I told you," Solar said as the light faded from Brant's hands.

"I told you so is not what I want to hear right now," Selene said still in awe by what just happened.

"Whoa!" Brant said looking up at Alpha. "What was that?" He asked trying to keep his composure.

"No, no, no. It's okay, bring it back," Alpha answered. Brant thought about it gradually rising from his hands and, just like it was obeying a command, it returned. He looked down at his hands to see the yellow light flow from one hand to the other, and his hands were bright yellow, almost translucent but not entirely. Brant stood taking deep breaths trying to figure out where this came from. He didn't have this when he unintentionally left home, but now, he had it. Brant tried putting the pieces together. After he opened the portal, he came here and nothing happened in between, or something did? He thought about everything that happened but, since his eyes were closed for the answer, this only created more questions.

"I knew it," Kit whispered to herself with a smile. Brant looked down at his hands as the light faded away.

"Sorry," he said looking over at Alpha and Kit.

"Don't be," Kit replied, then they looked over at Selene.

"Let's go outside and sit," she said looking at the floor.

13

BRANT FOLLOWED EVERYONE OUTSIDE and over to a small sitting area just by the front door underneath the awning. They all sat down facing each other in a circle. As Brant sat down next to Kit and Solar, he could see everyone wanted to know more as Alpha sat next to his sister and Selene sat opposite Brant.

"What's your name again?" Selene asked. She didn't take anyone said before seriously but that was different now.

"Brant Wilson," he answered.

"Where you from?" She asked.

"San Francisco," Brant answered.

"What planet is that on?" Alpha asked. Brant didn't think about naming the planet, but he was way out of his comfort zone, so he just kept going with it.

"Earth," he answered.

"That's a stupid name for a planet," Solar added. Brant just chuckled not knowing what to say.

"Now, can someone tell me where I am?" He asked. "Is this the future?" Brant asked with a grin.

"What? No," Selene answered with a laugh. Brant smiled satisfied with the thought he got her to smile. "You landed in a world called Reavella," she answered.

"Is that a real word?" Brant asked.

"Of course, it is. She just told you," Solar answered.

"What I mean is, what is Reavella?" Brant corrected.

"A city full of creatures under the control of one man," Selene answered. Brant thought it was weird that that would be her answer; out of everything he saw, that was the thing she pointed out.

"It didn't used to be like that," Alpha added getting Brant's attention.

"What do you mean?" He asked. Alpha looked at Selene who gave him a nod of approval, then back at Brant.

"Not too long ago, there used to be a group of remarkable creatures that protected our world. We affectionately called them the Protectors," he started. "They were our first line of defense against invaders, until—" then, he stopped.

"Until, what?" Brant asked.

"Eclipse," Selene answered, taking over the story. "One day, he arrived with his armies and started to invade Reavella. The Protectors fought back but Eclipse's darkness was unlike anything seen before," she explained as everyone sat listening. "He conquered the city and hunted down every Protector he could find that challenged his rule, calling it *the Purge*."

"Including our family," Kit said looking at the ground. Brant looked over to see the two looking at the ground thinking the same thing.

"After the Purge, our family went into hiding, but we couldn't escape Eclipse's men," Alpha started. "They were captured but I followed them back to their base and snuck in to break them out. I was running out of time and my parents told me to save my sister, but they would have to stay behind," he said taking a deep breath. "We both escaped but never saw them again," Alpha said as Kit took his hand.

"Are you regretting that choice already?" She asked trying to lighten the mood.

"Of course not," Alpha said with a smirk. "I just knew I could've done more," he added.

"There was nothing else you could do," Kit said putting her head next to his.

"Thanks," he said with a smile.

"We've all lost someone we love," Solar said, getting Brant's attention. "I lost my fiancé to the dark king," he started. "Like the twins, we tried to live our life, but Eclipse found us anyway and killed her and left me for dead. I'm only alive by the grace of the light and the locals who found me and saved me before it was too late," he said lifting his shirt to reveal a scar where he was shot, then he put it back down.

"Sorry," Brant said looking at the three.

"We've all lost something," Selene started. "My father was killed right before the Purge. It was a taste of what was to come," she said but didn't go any farther. Brant wondered why she didn't go into detail like the others, but he wasn't about to go into a traumatic backstory right now. They were all the same age as him but have gone through so much.

"I lost my parents, too," Brant said catching everyone by surprise, but he just continued. "But my story isn't as traumatic as yours," he said with a grin trying to lighten the mood. "My father took one look at me and decided he did not want me," he explained. "Can't say I'm the most popular guy around either, most people view me as a reject. I guess the only difference between us is that you're wanted," Brant said with a chuckle.

"What about your mother?" Alpha asked.

"She left me, too," he answered but it was in a different tone as he looked down at the gray concrete.

"Well, if Eclipse finds out you have the light of Reavella, he'll come for you, too," Selene said looking at Brant.

"That's okay, my life was getting dull anyway," Brant joked. The others laughed a little as they looked around, but Brant could tell what they were thinking. He was out of his element, and he had no idea what he was up against, and he knew it; but at least he wasn't lying to himself.

"Selene," Solar said after looking at a watch on his right arm. "It's time."

"Good," she said standing up. "We'll finish this later," she said walking toward the pathway that Brant came in.

"Where are we going?" Brant asked as everyone started following.

"We have some business we have to attend to," Kit answered as Brant stood up.

"I didn't think I'd be working," he replied with a smirk as he started to walk up the rather steep hill.

"If you're going to stay, you're going to work," Selene said with a grin like she was happy with the thought of putting Brant to work. He looked over at the unique, young creature and smiled as they walked up the hill.

14

BRANT FOLLOWED THE GROUP of outcasts back to the train station. He watched them walk in and head toward the back of the train as they opened a sliding door to reveal a group of gray metal crates. Solar jumped up and into the car of the train. He stepped next to the closest crate and pressed a small red button on the side. The metal crate started floating, so whoever was moving it could do it way easier than lifting. Solar gently pushed the first crate over to Alpha who was waiting for his load. He grabbed the crate, pushed it out of the train, and started walking toward the door while Solar got another crate and handed it to Selene, then to Kit, as Brant watched not knowing what they were up to.

"What's in the crates?" Brant asked as Alpha walked by.

"If I told you I'd have to kill you," Alpha answered with a smirk.

"That joke's still not funny," he replied when Selene walked by.

"Don't worry, nothing's going to hurt you . . . yet," she said looking at Brant out of the corner of her eye.

"That was supposed to make me feel better?" Brant asked himself as Kit stepped up.

"Grab a crate, pull your weight," she said, following Alpha and Selene. Brant looked over at the door where the three waited. He took a deep breath and walked over to the train where Solar was getting another container. He looked with a smirk and handed him a crate. Brant pulled the crate out of the train and placed it on the ground as it bounced once or twice still floating a few inches off the ground. He pushed the crate toward the door while Solar grabbed one last crate and closed up the train. It was easier to move than what Brant was expecting but it still had some weight to it. He walked up standing next to Selene as Solar met up just behind him.

"Is that everything?" Selene asked making sure they were ready to go. Solar nodded yes as they stood inside the wooden archway. "Let's go," she said as she started walking pushing the crate. Brant followed the group as they walked down the center pathway making their way back down the hill. Brant looked around at more homes the size of small trailers, but they looked like normal homes with front lawns, windows with shutters, and flower beds by the front door.

"What is this place?" Brant asked.

"The locals call it *The Hidden*," Alpha answered.

"A small village full of people who are wanted by Eclipse for having the light and wanting to live a simple life after they stood up to him for what they believe, or even just saying a sentence against him," Kit added.

"Most of these people we helped ourselves," Solar said as they walked down the hill toward the small pond at the bottom of the hill.

"Why?" He asked.

"Because it's the right thing to do," Selene answered looking at Brant wondering why he would ask a question like that.

"No, I mean why would you risk your life for total strangers?" Brant clarified. "If you're being hunted more than everyone here, why not just hide out?"

"You don't believe in fighting a fight greater than you?" Selene questioned back.

"Not something I would sign up for," he answered. They all looked at each other a little disappointed, but none of them knew the things Brant had gone through and the real reason why he believed it.

"You'd be surprised how good it feels," Selene said as they walked up to the pond. Brant just let it go as they all started to line up with their backs to the small body of water. Brant turned around facing the three hills of The Hidden as creatures started coming out of their homes.

"Who wants free grub?" Alpha yelled as everyone came out. They all opened the lids to their crates to see them full of food. Brant looked at their crates with a surprised look on his face. He opened his crate to see it stocked full of food. The food resembled food from his world but was different. The bread looked blue and there was an apple but it was the size of a mango and smelled more like a strawberry. Brant looked up to see the street getting crowded as everyone came out. He looked over to see everyone smiling and talking with others as they handed out food. "Hey, how are you?" Alpha asked handing out food.

"How'd your week go?" Kit asked as Brant overheard their conversation.

"This looks good," a villager said walking up to Solar.

"Yes, it does, doesn't it?" Solar said with a gentle grin. Brant looked up from his crate. He watched everyone grab food; from small children to adults, they grabbed with a smile on their faces. Brant watched a bear come over dressed in jeans and a long-sleeved shirt full of holes and grab a piece of fruit from the container.

"Thank you, thank you so much," he said putting his hand on Brant's shoulder before he walked away.

"I didn't do anything," Brant said quietly feeling guilty having him thinking it. He watched more creatures come and take food when a small raccoon girl walked up with her mother and took a piece of fruit then reached in for another.

"Oh, no, honey, just one," the mother said. Brant looked down at the fruit, and then at the little girl as she placed the second fruit back in the container. He reached and grabbed another fruit and handed it down to the little girl.

"Don't tell anyone," Brant whispered as he winked at the kid. She laughed as she took the fruit.

"Thank you," the mother said as Brant stood back up. He nodded as the two started to leave but the girl looked back and waved at Brant before rounding the corner. He smiled and waved back as more creatures surrounded the only human in the crowd. Brant smiled as he started to reach in and grabbed the fruit for the people.

"Here you go," he said getting into it and enjoying himself. "How are you?" Brant asked handing out food. Kit looked over at Brant hearing the sound of his voice to see him smiling as he handed out the rest of the fruit.

"Hey," she whispered to Selene standing next to her.

"What?" Selene asked looking over at Kit. Kit motioned her head toward Brant. She watched as he handed out the food still with a smile on his face.

"Imagine that," Selene said with a smirk. "He'll get on I told you so," she said with a smile. She looked over at Brant again as they handed out the rest of the food as the three moons of Reavella hung in the night sky.

15

"WE HAD A GOOD turnout," Kit said as they walked back into the train station with their crates empty. "What'd you think, Brant?" She asked.

"It was fun," he answered.

"I told you so," Selene said with a smile.

"You did," Brant replied with a laugh. He took in his empty crate and placed it along the wall with the others.

"So, why do you quote, unquote not like to help people?" Alpha asked as they stood in the station.

"Long story," he answered.

"Well, I'm too tired to invest in a long story," Kit said as she started to walk to the door.

"Same," Solar agreed. Brant smiled and shrugged his shoulders as he started to follow everyone out. He turned around to see the train car still full of crates from a window just to the side of the door.

"So, all those crates are full of food?" Brant asked.

"Yep," Alpha answered.

"Huh," Brant replied turning around. "I was hoping you'd have another golden orb thing," he said. Everyone stopped and looked at each other hoping they didn't hear Brant right.

"What?" Selene asked.

"Yeah, it's a small ball," he explained. "That's how I got here in the first place. I accidentally opened it and fell through a blue hole and ended up here," Brant said, looking over at Selene who had a look of fear in her eyes.

"Where is it?" She asked.

"I don't know, I dropped it when those weird armored freaks were chasing me," Brant answered. They all looked at each other like Brant just confessed he committed a terrible crime.

"Who opened it?" Alpha asked in the same worried tone as Selene.

"I did," Brant answered. "Why, what was it?" He asked. They all just looked at each other not giving him an answer.

"It's too late to go to the valley tonight," Selene said to the others.

"Tomorrow?" Kit asked.

"Tomorrow morning," she answered.

"Can someone tell me what I did wrong?" Brant asked not knowing what he did.

"Nothing, just the sky is going to fall," Selene answered.

"That's a good one," Brant started to say but realized she wasn't joking. "That wasn't a joke," he said biting his lip as everyone started to walk out of the station. "Sorry," he said apologizing.

"It's okay you didn't know," Selene replied as they started to walk back to the house.

"I mean I still don't know but that's okay, I guess," Brant said with a grin.

"Hurray, for ignorance," Selene joked making everyone laugh.

"Okay, that one I liked," Brant said as he laughed.

"Nothing like a passive–aggressive joke to lighten the mood," Alpha said with a yawn. "But I'm going to bed."

"Same," Kit replied with a yawn.

"Come on you can bunk with me," Solar said putting one arm around Brant.

"Thanks, but I'll bunk on the couch if you don't mind," Brant said with a smile. He wasn't used to having interactions like this. He always wanted it but he didn't expect it to come from a group like this; he was still going to keep them an arm's length away just in case. They all walked underneath the awning and walked into the house as a pink figure came out from the bushes just behind the station. She walked up to the hill that Brant and the others just walked down looking over the village as she reached her bright pink hand in her pocket and pulled out a small, flat metal disk.

"Father," Darcy said, pushing a small button on the side. "I found them," she said with a cold smile.

16

ALL THE LIGHTS WERE turned off inside the small house as Brant stood in the living space.

"Everything's locked up," Selene said in a quiet tone since everyone, but her and Brant, were in bed. "You sure you want to bunk on the couch?" She asked.

"Yeah, I've slept on worse," Brant answered looking over the couch.

"Okay," she said with a laugh. Selene started to walk toward her room when Brant got her attention.

"Hey," he said making her turn around. "Thank you, for helping me."

"You're welcome," she replied with a soft grin.

"Truth be told, I thought you all were going to kill me," Brant said joking, but not entirely, at the same time.

"Yeah, we can be a little rough around the edges," Selene said walking back over to Brant still talking softly.

"I can't bash them too much, they helped me after all," he replied.

"Well, a lot of people trash us for trying to help," Selene said with a look like she had a few stories of some past experiences.

"Been there," Brant said raising his shoulders and looking over at the kitchen thinking of some instances himself. "But I guess I took the long way to tell you I appreciate what you've done for me," Brant said looking into her bright blue eyes.

"Anytime," she replied. "Now all we have to do is teach you how to use the light and you might go from flailing like a fish to almost making it out alive," Selene said with a smirk.

"You know you should write poetry," Brant said making her laugh. She looked down at the floor for a second or two then back at Brant.

"Get some rest, Brant," Selene said, then she turned back and headed toward her room. Brant watched her leave the room, then he turned around toward the couch. He laid down on the couch and he slid his head up by the arm. It wasn't the worst thing he'd ever laid on, but it wasn't the most comfortable either. He moved his shoulders trying to get comfortable as everything stood in silence. Brant lay there trying to get his brain to turn off but after everything that happened it was hard to think of anything else. He looked out the window through a small opening in the shade to see three moons hanging in the sky. His eyes started to feel heavier and heavier, and soon after he fell asleep.

17

ALL WAS QUIET, BOTH outside and inside, as the hidden village was fast asleep. Brant lay on his back in a deep sleep when his body started to get cold. He turned over on his side trying to get warm but he couldn't, it felt like someone was running the AC and he was right by the air vent. Brant opened his eyes and sat up still with a cold feeling, looking around but nothing was there. Suddenly he heard a voice outside yell.

"Move!" Someone shouted. Brant shot around and looked out the window. He looked to the side of the road and saw dark armored ravens walking up to the house next to them, opening the door, and getting everyone out as they searched.

"What's going on?" Kit asked as she and Alpha ran out of the hallway still in the same clothes.

"The Dark Army's found us," Solar answered walking out of his room.

"How?" Kit asked.

"I don't know," Alpha answered as Selene walked out still wearing the same outfits.

"The Dark Army's here," Solar explained as he walked over and looked out the window.

"I know, I felt it," she replied.

"Is that part of the light, too?" Brant asked as everyone stood by the window.

"Yes," she answered.

"Cool," Brant said knowing that an overcoming coldness was a normal feeling to them, but it was still foreign to him. Just as everyone stood by the window, there was a pounding on the door. They all turned around as the pounding continued.

"Plan A, or plan B?" Selene asked everyone.

"B," they all answered at the same time.

"Do I get a vote?" Brant questioned.

"No," Alpha answered rather quickly.

"That's fair," he replied as everyone's eyes never left the door.

"Open up!" The trooper yelled with two other officers standing behind him. He kept pounding as hard as he could but no one opened the white door.

"Break it down," the trooper ordered. The trooper stopped hitting the door with his fist, lowered his shoulder, and started to ram into it. With every hit, he could feel it come loose more and more till the lock broke and the door flew open. The trooper drew his blaster and ran inside with the second officer right behind him while the third guarded the door. They ran in to see Brant casually sitting on the couch.

"What's going on here?" The trooper asked Brant.

"You got me there, dude," Brant answered still having their undivided attention. Out of nowhere, Alpha ran out of the hallway that led to Selene's room and swung his hand like he was swinging a tennis racket as his hand lit up yellow. He swung his hand sending the trooper flying back like he was a pillow just as Solar ran out from behind the door. He grabbed the trooper's leg and pulled on it as hard as he could making it fall on his back, then as fast as he could reach his hand out, shot a bright yellow beam out of his furry hand and hit the trooper in the chest.

"There's still the trooper outside," Brant said still sitting on the couch. Solar turned toward the door and jumped out landing on the trooper before he could grab his weapon. Solar made a fist with his hand as it lit up yellow and swung down at the officer. He only hit the trooper once, but that was all that was needed to make the dark-armored soldier stop moving. Brant followed everyone outside as Solar stood up over the trooper.

"Remind me not to get on your bad side," Brant said with a grin.

"You're standing on my left side," Solar said with a literal tone.

"No, I mean—" he started to say but decided to just let it go. "Never mind."

"He takes everything literally," Alpha said as they stood underneath the covered area by the door. "Anything sarcastic goes over his head."

"Nothing goes over my head, my reflexes are too fast," Solar said as everyone looked at each other.

"I'm going to die," Brant said thinking this was going to be the end.

"We need to get the army's attention off the people and on us," Selene explained.

"How do we do that?" Brant asked.

"Just show our faces," Kit answered.

"We'll make our way down the hill, there's more room to fight by the pond," Selene added.

"Let's have some fun," Alpha said with a grin as he ran toward the pathway.

"Alpha, wait! Don't run in headfirst," Selene tried to explain but it was too late. He ran out of the shaded area just as two troopers walked by. He swung both his fists hitting the troopers and sending them flying back.

"He's insane," Brant said in disbelief.

"That's my brother," Kit said following his lead.

"Of course, he is your brother. You just now learned that?" Solar said running out.

"As I said, we can be a little rough around the edges," Selene said to Brant as she started to run toward the pathway. Brant followed her out just as a trooper pointed a blaster at her. She reached her hand out making the air around the trooper light up yellow and swung it to the left and, as if it was obeying a command, the trooper flew in the air in the same direction she moved her hand. Brant watched the trooper fly, then he looked back to see everyone slowly make their way down the hill fighting off the dark troopers as they went. He looked over at Kit just in time to see her jump up on a roof like she jumped on a trampoline and made it up with ease as she fought off a raven. Brant looked over at Solar and Alpha as they smashed the helmet of a trooper at the same time denting both sides. Brant turned around to see a trooper fire a dark purple blast at him.

"Whoa!" He shouted. Brant ducked just as the laser flew above his head. He looked up to see Selene hit the trooper in the back and shot down at him taking him out.

"What are you doing?" She asked running up to him. "Fight back."

"I don't have a weapon," he answered. Selene rolled her eyes and reached down and grabbed Brant's hand and placed it on his chest.

"You are one," Selene said with a grin, then, she ran down the hill to help the others. Brant watched her run down the hill, and then he looked down at his hand as he raised it to eye level. He opened his hand and concentrated just like he did earlier and his hand lit up yellow after it flickered once or twice.

"Here we go," he said to himself as he started to run down the hill.

18

BRANT RAN DOWN THE hill meeting up with the others. Just as they reached the bottom where it started to level out a trooper yelled from behind him.

"Halt!" He yelled. Brant turned around to see the troopers with their blasters drawn. "Don't move!" They ordered. Brant looked back at the others as they fought in time to see Kit fire a beam of light from her hand, and then he looked back at the troopers as they started to walk up to him.

"Ha ha," Brant laughed as he reached his hand out but nothing happened. The trooper stopped expecting something to happen as they lowered his blaster in confusion. "Hold on," he said putting his hand down and looking it over. "Sorry, I'm new at this," Brant said hitting his hand like that would have done the trick. As he stood there he thought about the light inside the tunnel for a brief moment and, apparently, it was enough. Suddenly Brant's hands lit up yellow making him jump back not ready for that outcome. "Got it!" Brant said proudly. The troopers raised their blasters and opened fire on Brant. He ducked as the first shot sped over him. Brant stood up and swung his hand toward the trooper as a bright beam shot out. It sped through the air but missed. The trooper stepped to the side and opened fire again. Brant stepped to the side and swung his hand making a bright beam of light appear. It sped through the air just like the first time but this time it hit its target. The trooper fell to the ground after the shot connected with his chest.

Brant looked down at the trooper, lifeless on the ground, then at his hand. He felt guilty about it but what was he supposed to do? Brant turned around and faced the pond so he didn't have to look at the trooper on the ground. He turned around to see the others make their way toward the pond where they had given out the food only a few hours ago. He started to run over but stopped when he heard a little girl scream. Brant looked over to his left to see the small raccoon girl he helped earlier and her mother with a trooper pointing his blaster at the two. Brant looked over at everyone biting his lip. He'd be safe with the others but he couldn't live with himself if he just left them for dead.

"Brant, come on!" Selene yelled, but Brant ran in the other direction. "What are you doing?!" She yelled watching everything. Brant jumped up high in the air, higher than what he was expecting.

"Whoa, whoa, whoa!" Brant said as he started to fall back to the ground getting everyone's attention. "Oh, yeah, coming at you from the sky," he said as he flew down expecting to land on the trooper, but overshot his mark. He landed three feet away from the dark trooper landing on his face. "Okay," Brant said in pain as he stood up and everyone watched Brant fall on his face.

"Oh, wow!" Kit said as they watched Brant get to his feet.

"Can you guys pretend that didn't happen?" He asked as he rubbed his head for a moment. The trooper held his blaster up and opened fire at Brant who was not amused by his attempt to play off his fall. Brant swung his hand out trying to fire a beam of light, but something different happened. A bright yellow disk appeared hovering over the palm of his hand with a small pattern that surrounded the edges like a shield. The soldier's dark purple shot bounced perfectly off the shield and sped back to him hitting him in the neck and sending him to the ground. Brant lowered his hand as the shield faded away. "I did not mean to do that," he said with a smile looking at the little girl. She laughed as Brant started to run past them. "Get to a safe area," he said running past them.

"Thank you," the mother said as Brant ran by. He looked out of the corner of his eye to see the two running in the other direction as he made his way to the others.

"Nice job," Selene said with a grin pretending they didn't see him fall flat on his face.

"Really?" Brant asked.

"Yeah, it's not every day we watch someone fall on his face like that," Alpha answered.

"Alpha," Kit said hitting her brother in the shoulder.

"What? He did," he defended.

"The light is designed to protect you from serious blows but it would seem you found the dreaded in-between," Solar explained.

"Well, if anyone would find it, it would be me," Brant said with a grin. "Now what?" He asked.

"We have an escape plan just in case something like this would ever happen," Selene answered. "Head over to the trees that intertwine," she said pointing to the far right. Brant looked over to see two trees with two stumps but as the two grew their branches became intertwined.

"What's over there?" Brant asked.

"If we told you, would it bring you closer?" Kit asked sarcastically.

"No," Solar answered not realizing it was sarcastic.

"Can we focus please?" Selene said getting everyone back on track. "We have to get out of here."

"What about everyone else?" Brant questioned as everyone started to move toward the trees.

"We created an escape plan for everyone just in case this would happen," Selene answered.

"At this point, everyone should be safe," Alpha added as they ran.

"Wow, you guys like to plan, don't you?" Brant asked with a grin as they ran.

"We are expert planners," Solar said in his deep voice. Brant just smiled as he ran with these creatures. They ran past the center street and made their way to the third street when a line of troopers round around the corner blocking the road.

"Whoa!" Selene said as they stopped. Then, they turned around to see another group of soldiers line up and block the road boxing the outlaws in.

"Great," Alpha whispered to himself as they looked around. The soldiers lined up and pointed their weapons at the group as the small fountain at the center of the pond filled the dead noise. Just as everyone stood still not knowing where to go next, a new figure walked behind the line of soldiers. They separated just enough for her to walk through as she stepped into the blockade.

"Well, well, well, what do we have here?" She asked making Brant turn around. His eyes got wide to see a girl with light pink translucent skin, pink hair, and a dress. "The whole gang's here," Darcy said with a grin.

"Darcy," Selene said with a sigh.

"Is that a—?" Brant started to ask himself not believing his eyes as the stranger continued.

"You have been quite the busy rebel haven't you, Selene?" Darcy asked.

"What are you doing here?" Selene questioned back, never taking her eyes off her.

"Well, when we heard you had a shiny new toy I just had to come and check it out for ourselves," Darcy answered. "Say where is he?" She asked. Darcy looked around at the group going over each one till her eyes met Brant's at the end of the line. "It's a human?" She asked.

"Hi," Brant said with an awkward wave.

"Hey, he's cute," Darcy said with a smile looking over Brant. "I can see why you want to keep him to yourself."

"Is that a ghost?" Brant whispered to Alpha.

"Yes. I mean, we think so," he answered as Darcy continued.

"You have a name, human?" Darcy asked Brant but Selene stepped in.

"He's not giving you anything," she said defensively. Brant looked at Selene wondering why she got so tense all of a sudden. This wasn't any worse than before but she was on the defensive for some reason.

"Oh, I'm sorry I forgot to acknowledge the beloved leader," Darcy snapped back.

"What do you want anyway?" Selene asked as the situation was getting more and more intense by the second.

"The dark king requests the human's presence," she answered.

"Why?" Selene questioned.

"You know why," Darcy answered with a cold smile. Selene looked at the young ghost taking a deep breath. "Talk about a blast from the past."

"It's not that far in the past," Selene replied.

"Feels like yesterday," Darcy added. Brant looked at the two wondering what they were even talking about. It was like they were talking about someone or something but they didn't have to go into details, although he wished they would so he'd know what was going on. "Surrender, now," she ordered getting tired of the conversation.

"No," Selene said never taking her eyes off of the ghost.

"So, be it," Darcy said taking a step to the side. "Aim for everyone but the human," she ordered. The troopers tightened their grip on their weapons aiming for the group.

"Ready?" Selene whispered back to the others.

"Ready," Solar answered.

"What's the plan?" Alpha asked.

"Take out the troopers, I'll take Darcy," Selene answered as she stared at the ghost.

"What about me?" Brant asked.

"If Eclipse wants you, then he better not find you," Selene started. "Run!"

"Got it," Brant replied. He didn't like the thought of running while everyone else was fighting but, since he wasn't in any situation to argue, he went with it.

"The rest of you know what to do," Selene added.

"Ready!" Darcy yelled at the troopers.

"Get ready," Selene whispered.

"Aim!" She yelled as they got ready to fire.

"Here we go again," Kit whispered as the village stood in silence.

"Fire!" Darcy shouted giving the order.

19

"GET DOWN!" SELENE YELLED as the blast flew over their heads. Brant ducked just as the first shots flew over his head. "Brant, get safe," Selene said jumping to the side and dodging another shot. "I got Darcy," she said, then she took off after the ghost.

Brant took off toward the center road and started to run up the hill toward the station. He looked back out of the corner of his eye to see Selene run up to the ghost and everyone else left to fend for themselves. Brant ran up the hill passing small house after small house till he stopped about halfway to the top. He turned around and looked down at the street below seeing what they were up against. They went out of their way to help him and he was just going to run away? He bit his lip trying to convince his brain that it wanted to turn around and run toward the danger.

"I'm an idiot!" Brant yelled at himself. He turned around and bolted back down the hill as he saw more and more of the battlefield. He stopped at the bottom of the hill and looked around to see Kit and the others fighting off the last of the ravens, then over at Selene just standing in front of the ghost. He may not know what this was all about but he didn't like the thought of her fighting a ghost on her own. Brant took off back around the corner running as fast as he could toward Selene.

"Brant, what are you doing?" Kit asked not having a chance to follow with guards still surrounding the trio.

"I'm going to have my head examined," Brant answered as he ran.

"That doesn't make any sense? The psychiatrist lives on the other street," Solar said with a curious look. Brant ran around the corner passing a small swinging bench overlooking the pond as he got closer to Selene and the ghost. As he ran, he could hear a conversation between the two.

"Why do you have to make things so difficult?" Darcy asked with a whining voice. With all of her attention on Selene, she didn't see Brant running up behind her.

"We both had a choice," Selene answered, missing Brant running at her.

"I didn't," Darcy said with a deep sigh as her emotions started to pent up. She whipped her feet causing them to morph together and create a point as she hovered over the pathway like a typical ghost. "Ah!" She yelled flying toward Selene. Darcy swung her pointed feet at Selene like a whip. Selene jumped back and hurled a yellow beam at the ghost. "Ha ha ha," Darcy laughed as she separated her arms making her more translucent than usual for a few seconds as the beam flew through her.

"I hate it when you do that," Selene said looking up at the ghost. She jumped up eye level to Darcy and swung her fist all lit up with the light at her, but she leaned back as the blow missed her. Darcy straightened up as Selene started to fall toward the ground and swung her fist up hitting Selene in the chin. "Ah!" Selene said gritting her teeth. Then Darcy flew up higher than Selene was going, swung down hitting her on the head, and sent her flying to the ground. Selene landed hard on the pavement as a yellow shockwave spread on the pathway as if the light was protecting Selene from harm, but it still hurt as she stumbled to her knees.

"You were always the week one," Darcy said floating back down.

"Is that what you call restraint?" Selene asked still on her knees.

"You never had the nerve the do what needed to be done," Darcy answered slowly making her way to Selene.

"Eclipse thinks otherwise," she replied. Darcy clenched her fist and started to bend down to grab Selene by the throat when Brant ran up to the two.

"Hey!" He yelled getting their attention. Darcy turned around as Selene looked up to see Brant standing a few feet away.

"Brant," Selene whispered to herself thinking Brant had lost his mind.

"Have we met before?" He asked with a grin. Darcy looked down at Selene and then back up at Brant with a curious expression on her face. "I thought I saw you at Mickey's Not So Scary Halloween Party," he said with a smirk.

"What?" Darcy asked.

"Oh, it's a Halloween event down in Florida," Brant answered, taking a few steps closer as he stalled trying to get as close as he could. "It seemed like something you would get into."

"What does that have to do with any of this?" Darcy asked losing her patience.

"Nothing. I was just trying to get close to you so I can do this," Brant answered, throwing his hand out. Darcy lit up bright yellow as she flew back hitting the house behind her and cracking the white siding.

"Protector," Darcy said to herself as her eyes widened as far as they could in amazement. She pulled herself out of the wreckage and flew back toward Brant.

"Brant, get out of here," Selene said getting on one knee.

"I'm not afraid of a Halloween decoration," he replied as Darcy flew closer. "You should be the one getting safe," Brant added, then he took off running toward the ghost. He got down on his knees and slid like a soccer player as Darcy passed over him. He turned around and got to his knees and swung his bright yellow fist at her hitting her in the cheek sending her back and rolling on the ground till she stopped a few feet away. "I didn't mean to do that," Brant said with a grin looking at his hand as the yellow light faded. He looked up to see Darcy charging at him so he raised his hand and shot another beam out since it was the only thing he knew how to do on command. The beam shot through the air but Darcy was ready this time. She spread her arms out again and turned transparent again and the beam went right through her. "Oh, that's not right," Brant said as she swung her fist upward. Her fist met Brant's chin sending him upward with a yellow shockwave that protected him from a major blow, just like Selene, but he still felt it.

Darcy flew up, passing Brant, and swung down sending him back toward the ground. She flew underneath Brant and hit him to the side, then back up like she was juggling him as she just kept hitting him over and over in the air. She wiped her pointed feet at Brant hitting him in the stomach and sending him flying back. He hit the ground hard as a larger ring of light spread on the pavement where Brant hit, like when a drop hits a puddle and the ripples spread.

"That hurt but didn't at the same time," Brant said getting to his knees. Suddenly, Darcy sped down toward Brant.

"Get up, Brant!" Selene yelled. Brant looked up to see Darcy flying down. He rolled to the side just as Darcy landed her fist where his head was a few seconds ago. Darcy took the opening and flew at Brant swinging her fist at him again. Brant reached his arm up and opened his hand creating a shield like he unintentionally did before. Darcy's hand bounced off the shield.

"Ow!" Darcy said with a whine. She swung her fist at Brant again when he wasn't ready for it, hitting him in the cheek, then she swung again hitting the other side of his face. Brant fell on his back trying to step away but lost his footing and fell to the ground. He opened his eyes to see Darcy hovering over him, looking down at him with a cold smile. "Nowhere left to go," she said with a smile.

"True, but not for me," Brant replied with a smirk.

"Huh?" Darcy asked, but before Brant could answer, Selene kicked her in the face sending her back. Brant got to his feet and held his hand out stopping her midair as the air around her lit up yellow. Brant swung his hand to the water sending the young ghost girl in the same direction. She landed in the water as she tried her best to swim to shore. Darcy paddled to shore soaked to her ghostly bones, taking a deep breath after deep breath. She looked at her hand as it phased from solid to translucent and back as if her abilities were out of control due to the water.

"Not bad," Selene said stepping next to Brant.

"Thanks, I wasn't thinking," he joked.

"That was obvious," Selene said with a grin making Brant laugh. She looked at Brant and smiled, then over to see Kit, Alpha, and Solar running toward the trees. "Let's get out of here," she said running toward everyone else. Brant took off behind her as Darcy looked behind her to see them getting away, but she couldn't do a thing about it. Selene and Brant ran up to the corner just as the others arrived.

"Hey, he's still alive," Alpha said with a smirk.

"Not bad, human," Kit said with a smile as they started to run toward the arched tree.

"Thanks, I wasn't thinking much about what I was doing," Brant replied. "I think the adrenaline kicked in," he added.

"Definitely," Alpha said with a grin as they ran. The group ran underneath the archway and into a field of trees. Brant followed everyone around a series of corners as they ran who knows where. Brant ran around another tree line but stopped in amazement. There in the middle of the field stood what looked like a spaceship with a bright blue-and-white paint job.

"You've got to be kidding me," Brant said with a laugh of disbelief. He looked at the ramp that led inside just underneath a massive window that looked like the cockpit. Brant just stood there looking over the ship with its massive wings that spread out like an eagle.

"You coming or what?" Selene asked with a smile. Brant smiled in amazement as he followed the group inside.

20

ARCY CRAWLED OUT OF the bank still soaked from the water. She whipped her tail again making her feet reappear. She got to her feet and looked around at the empty village that was once full of people and troopers, but now sat empty with just her. Darcy reached into her pocket, pulled out a small flat disk, and pressed a small switch on the side. A few moments later, a hologram of Eclipse appeared in his black robe.

"Father," she said out of breath.

"Let me guess, they escaped?" Eclipse asked in his deep and oddly soothing voice.

"Yes," Darcy admitted.

"Did you at least get a look at who opened the orb?" He asked.

"Yes, it's a human," she answered.

"A human?" Eclipse asked not expecting that. "How interesting," he said rubbing his chin intrigued by this new development.

"There's something else, Father," Darcy said dreading this part. "He has the forbidden light."

"What?" He asked as he stopped rubbing his chin.

"He's untrained but stronger than he knows," Darcy explained.

"And Selene?" Eclipsed asked trying not to lose his composer.

"She's helping him, along with the other rebels," she answered.

"Did you at least get any of them?" He asked.

"No, sir," Darcy answered lowering her head for a moment or two.

"Which way did they go?" He asked.

"West," Darcy answered knowing she was on thin ice.

"How many ravens do you have?" Eclipse asked reaching the end of his rope.

"As I was—" Darcy started to answer but was cut off.

"Enough!" Eclipse yelled. "I'm coming there and I will deal with this band of outlaws myself!" He yelled, and then the image faded away. Darcy looked down at the flat disk and swallowed hard as everything stood in silence.

21

"**G**ET EVERYTHING READY FOR takeoff," Selene ordered as they walked into the ship. Brant walked up the ramp and into the ship. He looked around at the metal-grated area with five hammocks hanging on both sides of the ship and a table at the center of the room. He looked to the back of the room to see a stack of crates like the ones he carried before and a ladder that led up to the bridge.

"This is awesome!" Brant said geeking out about the thought that he was in something like a spaceship.

"Welcome aboard," Solar said with a grin while Kit and Alpha made their way up the ladder and into the bridge.

"Hey, that was the first time I could tell you were sincere," Brant replied as Selene walked over to the ladder.

"Don't tell me you're starting to learn," Selene said with a smile as Brant and Solar stepped up to the ladder.

"I could never," he replied with a grin.

"You did, too, I just heard you," Solar said as he climbed up the ladder. Brant smiled and shook his head as he watched Solar climb up. Just before he started to make his way up, he rubbed his hand over his cheek where he landed after being juggled by Darcy.

"Oh, here," Selene said seeing Brant rubbing his cheek. She turned around to a small cabinet just behind her and opened it to see what looked like a weird refrigerator full of food he'd never seen before. She reached to the back and pulled out something that looked like a green ice pack, turned back around, and handed it to Brant. "Here, use this."

"Thanks," Brant said taking the pack and stepping to the side of the ladder next to Selene as he placed the ice pack on his cheek.

"How do you feel?" Selene asked.

"Okay," he answered. "I thought I'd feel worse."

"I mean you took a beating," Selene said with a grin. "She just kept beating you senseless and you just got right back up," she said impressed. "You're so stubborn you don't know when to quit do you?"

"Well, I never thought of that as a good thing," Brant replied thinking of past instances in his life.

"It's a great thing, especially in our line of work," Selene said with a smile.

"Thanks, I . . ." Brant started to say when a voice came from above.

"Hey, Selene we're ready to go," Kit shouted down.

"Be right there," Selene replied as she stepped up to the ladder. "You coming?" She asked.

"I wouldn't miss this for anything," he answered placing the green ice pack back where it came from. He walked up to the ladder just as Selene made her way to the top. Brant climbed up to the bridge as he climbed up from the hole in the floor. He stood up and looked around. There were five seats with seatbelts that looked like they belonged in a fighter jet, but the seats had dark orange padding with each seat elevated so that it gave an unobstructed view of what's outside. He looked to the side of the seats to see a small digital panel, then he looked up to see the massive window that led out to the outside. "Whoa!" Brant said as he walked up to an empty seat.

"You might want to buckle up," Alpha said from what looked like the captain's chair with Kit sitting right beside him. Brant climbed up to the seat to the left. He sat down on the dark orange seat and started to fasten his seatbelt. He put it on like a backpack first one then the other, and then he fastened it with a metal clip that met at the center. Brant fastened his seat belt just as Selene jumped up to her seat.

"I thought I would be tired of asking this question but here we go," Brant said with a smirk. "Where are we going?"

"A valley a west of here," Selene answered.

"That cleared things up perfectly," Brant replied sarcastically having no idea what she was talking about. "Is it at least safe?"

"Yes, it's not on anyone's radar," Kit answered.

"But it's on yours?" He questioned.

"What's the matter? Don't trust us?" Alpha asked looking back at Brant for a moment, then he turned back around and pressed a series of switches.

"It's not a matter of trust, but I was just attacked by a ghost. So, I just want to know if I have to mentally get prepared for anything," Brant answered.

"Don't worry you're safe," Selene reassured. "Ready?" She asked Alpha.

"We're good to go," he answered.

"Take us there," Selene said giving him the okay. Alpha nodded and flipped a small red switch on the wall just by his seat. Suddenly, the ship started to move upward. Brant grabbed the arms of his seat with a death grip as the ship moved upward. Selene looked over at Brant who had a slightly terrified expression on his face as Alpha moved the joystick connected to the right arm of his chair to the left making the ship rotate. Brant smiled and took a deep breath as the shuttle evened out, facing the rest of the field of trees. Alpha reached to the right side of his seat, grabbed a small silver lever, and pushed it forward. The ship took off while Brant watched out the window as trees flew past them. He was terrified but loved every minute as they flew through the air.

B RANT STARED OUT THE window as they flew over a field of trees. He looked to his right to see the sun rising over the horizon.

"So, how long till we get there?" He asked.

"At this rate, we'll be there in about five minutes," Kit answered from the captain's chair.

"Make sure we're not being followed," Selene ordered.

"I've been monitoring the Dark Army's coms, and as of right now they don't know where we are," Solar explained from the row in front of Brant as he watched a small tablet connected to the arm of his chair.

"Good," Selene said while taking a deep breath, then it grew quiet as the engines propelled them through the air. Brant looked around at his surroundings, still taken back he was in such a cool ship. He looked down and studied the seat he was in. There was a small see-through tablet-like device on the right side of his seat, then he looked at the other arm to see a small cord that rose from the end of the seat. He reached inside his pocket where his phone still sat along with his EarPods. Brant pulled up his phone, but he had no cell service or reception of any kind. He figured that would be the case, but the fact he couldn't call for help from anyone where he was from still discouraged him a little. He looked at the bottom of his phone, then at the cord's end to see the shapes line up. Brant reached down and pushed the cord into the phone. The cord's tip was smaller than Brant's phone but he wiggled it in till the battery light lit up green. Brant sat the phone down and sat back in his seat when, suddenly, music started playing. Everyone started to look around as a guitar started to play through the ship's PA system.

"What is that?" Alpha asked from the pilot's seat.

"Oh, sorry. I didn't realize that would start to play," Brant said as he reached for his phone to turn off the music. "I should've known all my downloaded music would play."

"No, no, no. Let it go," Selene said getting Brant's attention. "I've always wanted to listen to music," she said looking at the phone. Brant looked at her taken back by the fact she never had heard music before. He just sat back as the song started with just a simple guitar melody.

"*My arms are tired and weary, these wounds are on full display. I've tried every door in the hallway, there's just nowhere that I feel safe,*" the song sang as the drums came in. "*I see the light but never find the surface, I don't know if I can swim no more. White knuckles and wild horses. One day we'll wash up on Mercy's shore, one day we'll wash up on Mercy's shore.*" They all listened as Brant started to sing along just as the song started quietly go down.

"*Ooh, oh-oh-oh-oh, oh- oh- oh- oh, oh- oh- oh- oh,*" Brant sang with his eyes closed. Kit turned around just as Selene looked over at Brant and smiled softly as everyone started to get into the song when the lead singer started to sing with the drums and guitar getting louder again and creating the beat.

"*I'm lost in the waves that crush me, they bring discovery where darkness hides. Just over the ridge in front of you, another mountain that you'll have to climb,*" the male artist sang as everyone started to bob their heads with the music but Brant was the only one singing with it.

"This is pretty good," Kit said looking over at Alpha who nodded his head in agreement while the song repeated the chorus.

"*I see the light but never find the surface, I don't know if I can swim no more. White knuckles and wild houses. One day we'll wash up on Mercy's shore, one day we'll wash up on Mercy's shore,*" the song blared inside the ship as Brant sang along, but this time it wasn't just him.

"*Oh whoa, whoa, whoa, Oh, whoa, whoa,*" they all started to sing along but not as loud as Brant, who didn't hear them over the music. The music started to quiet down again as they led into the bridge with just the guitar playing.

"*We're a child in the car asleep, in the driveway at night. Our mother's gonna slowly sneak our body inside. We can rest in the arms of trust. There's no way we can say we've earned our way into the light, all we have to do is stay,*" Selene listened to the words as she looked down at the floor. Thinking about the lyrics as the song started to pick up again with the chorus. "*I see the light but never find the surface, I don't know if I can swim no more. White knuckles and wild horses. One day we'll wash up on Mercy's shore, one day we'll wash up on Mercy's shore,*" then, suddenly, they all started to shout at the top of their lungs singing along.

"*Oh, whoa, whoa, whoa, Oh, whoa, whoa, whoa!*" They all shouted getting Brant's attention. He looked around to see everyone singing to the music. Brant looked around with a smile on his face to see Alpha and Kit singing in the front seats, even Solar was going at it. He looked to his left to see Selene closing her eyes and singing along with a smile on her face as the song started to fade out. Brant looked around as he reached for his phone and turned off the music as rock structures started to come into view in the distance.

"I liked that," Kit said as it got quiet in the giant cockpit again.

"Thank you," Brant said with a smile. He wasn't used to having people sing along and get into music as much as him, but it was a breath of fresh air for him.

"What other songs do you have?" Alpha asked.

"Oh, I have a bunch of songs on here," he answered looking at his phone. "I love music, so I like to listen to it as much as possible."

"It was nice to hear a melody again," Solar said in a soft tone.

"I'm glad I can help," Brant replied with a smile as Selene looked at the floor again thinking about the lyrics of the song.

"What's the song called?" Kit asked.

"*Mercy's Shore* by NEEDTOBREATHE," he answered.

"I liked it," Kit said with a grin as they flew through the air. As they sped through the sky, Selene looked over at Brant.

"Brant," she said in a soft tone. Brant looked over to see a look of worry in her eyes he'd never seen before. "I . . . I'm—" she started to say, but she had trouble getting whatever was on her mind out, then she was cut off from the front row.

"We're here," Alpha said from the front seat. Selene looked out the window to see a line of rocks a few yards away.

"Good," she said, taking a deep breath with something on her mind but couldn't get it out.

23

THE SHIP FLEW UP to a line of bright tan rocks that rose from a body of water that divided the field of trees and the rock formations. Brant looked out the window to see Alpha navigate around pillars of boulders that rose to the sky.

"Cool," he said with a smile as the ship turned around the boulders.

"Hold on," Alpha said with a smirk as the ship leveled out. Brant watched as an opening came into view carved out of the rocks.

"Wait, you can't be serious?" Brant said looking at the opening that didn't look large enough for the ship to fit through.

"I told you to hang on," Alpha replied fighting back a smile to make it sound believable. Brant grabbed the arms of his chair as they flew closer and closer to the opening. He leaned back in his seat as the opening sped closer, but it wasn't getting bigger as they flew up to it.

"Hey, hey, hey!" Brant yelled as they flew inside the hole in the rocks. Everybody turned around to look at Brant who had a panicked look spread across his face thinking they were going to collide with the rocks and started to laugh at him. Brant took a few deep breaths as everyone laughed. He looked over at Selene who officially lost it. "That was cruel," he said with a chuckle.

"You looked like you were terrified," Kit said with a smile.

"I was," he replied. "And the sad thing is you all thought it was funny," Brant said with a smile.

"Your pathetic screams were amusing," Solar said with a grin.

"I'm glad I can make you smile," Brant said with a grin as the ship flew through the rocks. Brant looked up to see the rockwork above the window just barely missing the panel of windows. He looked ahead to see sunlight shining at the other end of the tunnel. Alpha started to pull a lever on the right side of his seat back making the ship slow down. The ship slowed down as it gradually flew through the other end of the tunnel with a landing pad made of white concrete that sat with two waterfalls on both sides of the tunnel they had just flown through. Alpha gradually pulled the steering mechanism down and flipped a small switch on the wall next to him causing the landing gear to come down. The ship landed and bounced once or twice as it settled.

"Nice landing," Kit said looking at her brother.

"Was there ever any doubt?" He asked.

"Some," Selene answered with a grin.

"That was the best landing I've ever experienced," Brant said.

"Thank you," Alpha said looking at Brant.

"I mean that was the first landing I've ever gone through so take that for what it is," he added. Everybody laughed again as Alpha just looked at Brant with a smirk.

"Very funny," he replied. "Now, get off my ship."

"That's fair," Brant said with a laugh as they all made their way off the ship and onto the rocky terrain. He climbed down the ladder and back into the main living area within the ship just as the ramp extended down letting light pour inside. Brant walked out first with everyone following behind. He looked around to see tall tan rocks towering all around, then up ahead to see two pathways that separated. He looked down to see the platform they landed on. It was made of white cement just like a helipad from his world, but with a spaceship sitting right behind him which made it way more impressive. He turned around and looked up at the two waterfalls, one on each side of the elevated platform.

"Pretty cool, huh?" Kit asked as they walked off.

"Yeah," he answered looking up at the towering boulders.

"We better keep moving," Selene said getting everyone's attention. "Alpha, Solar, Kit, you three head down the left path," she explained, motioning to the splitting pathway up ahead. "Brant and I will head down the right path."

"Wait, why would we spit up?" Alpha asked.

"I'll tell you when you're older," Kit said grabbing her brother's arm and started walking. She turned around and winked at Selene while Brant looked back at the crystal-clear waterfalls. Selene smiled and winked back as Brant turned back around having no clue what happened behind his back.

"So, are you going to pretend we didn't just see that?" Solar asked as he followed.

"Can we please not ruin the tender moment we just had," Kit answered as they walked around a tree and down the pebble pathway.

"What was that about?" Brant asked.

"Who knows," she answered. "Come on, let's get going," Selene said as she started to walk with Brant right behind her.

24

THE TWO STARTED TO walk down the pebble pathway as the sounds of the waterfalls faded away in the background. Brant looked around at his new surroundings. They were walking along a cliff with a wall of rocks on his right and a sharp drop on his left. He looked down to see crystal-clear water flowing down a river and trees that grew up where the water splashed around, but their leaves were bright blue. As they walked Selene looked over at Brant while he was looking at the river and straightened her blond hair just a little as she walked.

"You did a good job back there," she said trying to get a conversation started.

"Aside from falling on my face," Brant added.

"You almost didn't. No one gets used to these abilities right away," Selene said trying to make Brant feel better.

"How many tries did it take you?" Brant asked wondering how good of a job he did. Selene just looked at him with her ears raised not expecting that question.

"Oh, so many. I was not good at it, worse than you," she answered and smiled at Brant trying to make him feel better about falling on his face in front of everyone.

"You got it right away, didn't you?" Brant questioned again seeing right through what she was saying.

"I got it right away, but I was raised here," Selene answered.

"Right, now you're just trying to make me feel better," Brant said with a smirk as they walked.

"What, no," Selene said denying everything she just said. "Is it working?" She asked.

"Little bit, yeah," Brant answered with a smile. She fought back a smile as she looked over at Brant for a moment then looked straight ahead before Brant realized she was looking at him. He looked over at Selene just as she looked ahead to see the sun bounce off her bright blond hair. "Can I ask you something?" He asked.

"Sure, why not," Selene answered with a smirk.

"Where are you from?" Brant asked. "Everyone here resembles something from my world. Granted it's a very small resemblance but you all are unlike anything I've ever seen before," he clarified so Selene wouldn't get the wrong idea.

"I don't know where I'm from," Selene answered.

"Really?" Brant asked surprised.

"Yeah," Selene answered. "My first memory is arriving in Reavella with my father. I remember landing in a strange new world while I was holding my father's hand. We walked out and he told me we would be okay as long as we had each other, but that all changed," she explained.

"Eclipse?" Brant asked.

"Yeah," she answered looking at the ground. "After he killed my father, I went into hiding after I discovered I somehow got the light just by stepping foot here, and not long after I met the others."

"Sorry," Brant apologized.

"It's okay. By doing this I feel like it makes up for everything else," Selene said still looking at the ground. Brant thought that was a weird thing to say. She was being honest with him. There was still something else she wasn't telling him, but he figured he wasn't going to get it unless she wanted to tell him on her own.

"Anything I can do to help?" Brant asked hoping he might be able to help.

"I thought you didn't like helping others?" Selene questioned back.

"Well," Brant said, debating whether or not he should share his past that he didn't like to relive, but she was honest with him to a certain extent, so he might as well be truthful with her. "After my father left me at the orphanage, I tried to make some friends so I wasn't alone in the world, but everyone knew what happened to me. They called me names like a reject, or a mistake of the human race. Then I tried helping others where I could, but with everything I did the people I was helping expected the worst, so they would kick me out of whatever I was doing, blaming me for their mistakes," he said as Selene listened without saying a word. "That's a pretty lame excuse, huh?" Brant asked with a grin trying to lighten the mood.

"Well, I'm glad you're here," Selene said with a soft smile. Brant looked over at her and smiled back as the pathway started to work its way downward.

"Anyway," Brant said looking around at something to change the subject. "Wow, that's clear water!" he said looking down at the river.

"Brant, I'm glad you told me," she said still looking at him with the same smile. Brant looked back and nodded as they started to walk down the hill and to the left where the pathway connected again, but as they rounded the corner a new site came into view. Built in between the rocks was a small village with supports raising everything above the water just a few feet below.

"What is this place?" Brant asked looking down at the village.

"The Valley of Light," Selene answered. "See why it's not on anyone's radar?" She asked back.

"It's beautiful," Brant answered looking down at the village suspended above the purified water.

"It is," she agreed. "Come on, we better get going," she said walking down the hill where the pathway connects before it led into the village.

"Why are we here?" Brant asked as he followed by her side.

"I need to talk to someone here," Selene answered.

"Seems like a long trip just to talk to someone," Brant replied as the pathway leveled out and the pathway connected.

"Yes, but we can't just call anyone, that defeats the point of being undetectable," she replied. "Besides, this is important."

"Well, if it helps me get home," Brant said. Selene looked at Brant and took a deep breath forgetting that was the point of why he was coming in the first place. With everything going on, she forgot why he was there to begin with, but she just let it go for the time being when, suddenly, they heard voices behind them.

"That doesn't explain why we had to split up," Alpha said as they walked down the pathway.

"What if you wanted to go on a walk with someone?" Kit asked.

"Which would never happen," he answered back as they walked up to Brant and Selene.

"Oh, shut up," Kit said putting an end to the conversation as they met up.

"What's going on?" Brant asked.

"Oh, just trying to have a conversation with my naïve brother," Kit answered.

"I'm not being naïve, just practical," Alpha said with a shrug.

"Was he?" Brant asked Solar.

"I prefer to remain neutral in such matters," he answered.

"Can we focus, please," Selene said getting everyone's attention.

"Are you sure he's expecting us?" Kit asked Selene.

"Knowing this old geezer, he's been ready for us for a month," Alpha answered before she could.

"Who?" Brant asked.

"I would explain it to you but I don't think you'll believe me," Selene answered with a grin as she started to walk over to an arched bridge that stretched over the water connecting the gravel-like path to the planks and bamboo walkways that stood over the water.

"At this point, I don't think anything would surprise me," Brant replied.

"You'd be surprised," Selene said with a deep breath as everyone walked over the pathway and into the valley.

25

THEY WALKED UNDERNEATH A small rock archway that acted as an entrance to the village. Brant looked around at the suspended town as he walked on bamboo logs tied together with a green rope holding everything in place. He looked up to his right to see a rock wall higher than most skyscrapers in San Francisco with small openings scattered all around allowing water to fall through. Brant looked forward again looking over more bamboo houses as he walked.

"Why did they build a town like this here?" Brant asked as they walked.

"There used to be a thousand of these villages scattered all over this side of the world, but when Eclipse came he tried to shut them all down," Alpha answered.

"Why?" Brant questioned as he looked around.

"The people here used to mine for Ranium, a special element used to power ships, but Eclipse didn't want a ton of resources at the citizen's disposal so he destroyed all of them except for this one," he explained.

"Why did he leave this one alone?" Brant asked.

"This valley was located far away from the other colonies. Either he missed it or didn't care to level this one to the ground and, believe it or not, this is the smallest of them all," Alpha answered as they all walked over an arched bridge.

"I hope I never have to meet Eclipse," Brant replied as they walked away from the bridge.

"Believe me, you're not missing anything," Kit said as they continued walking through the valley. The group walked past more homes suspended above the water by a few skinny poles as they made their way to a larger structure at the back of the valley that had a set of stairs that led up to the front entrance. Brant looked straight ahead to see a girl with brown hair waiting for them.

"Hey, guys," she said meeting up with the group. Brant looked over at the new stranger as she got closer. She had a green dress on that popped off her bright brown fur and dark green eyes. Brant looked over her to try to think of what she looked like. She looked like a chipmunk or a squirrel if they were tall and walked with two legs.

"Seems like I'm always thanking you for something," Selene said reaching her hand out.

"I'd be disappointed if you didn't," the stranger replied shaking her hand. "I hear there's a new member to the team. Where is he?" She asked. Selene looked behind her to see Brant. "That's him?"

"That's him," Selene answered as the girl walked up to Brant.

"A human?" She asked Selene looking over Brant from top to bottom.

"Yep," Selene answered.

"Hi?" Brant said with a little hesitation as the girl circled him. "And you are?" He asked.

"Oh, right sorry," she said realizing she forgot to introduce herself. "I'm Crystal," she introduced herself.

"I'm Brant," he said reaching his hand out. "Nice to meet you," Brant said shaking her hand.

"Same," Crystal said with a smile.

"What are you a sheep?" Brant asked not having a clue what this creature was.

"Do sheep look like me where you come from?" She questioned back with a chuckle.

"What, no!" Brant said, not expecting her to come back at him that quick. "What I meant to say is what are you?" He clarified.

"We're what they call Miners," Crystal answered. "I guess you can say we're in a group all our own."

"Like the Protectors?" Brant asked.

"He's a fast learner," Crystal answered looking back at Selene.

"I thought you said nothing would surprise you?" Alpha asked sarcastically.

"I probably should stop saying that," he replied with a grin.

"Well, the five of you have been around, haven't you?" Crystal asked as they stood a few feet from the set of stairs that led up to the large building.

"Just like any other day," Kit answered.

"Yeah, except now you have that—" Crystal said pointing at Brant.

"Why is she talking to me like I'm a pet?" He asked Solar.

"I don't know. Maybe 'cause you're acting like one," he answered.

"Oh," Brant said then he realized what Solar meant. "What?" He asked as the conversation around the group moved on.

"We need to talk to the chief," Selene said.

"What's up?" Crystal asked. "Is it about that thing?" She asked gesturing toward Brant.

"I'm standing right here," Brant interjected.

"Yes," Selene answered.

"He might have brought something with him," Kit added.

"Might?" Alpha said looking at his sister with a questioning look. "How else do you think he got here?"

"I was giving the situation the benefit of the doubt," Kit replied.

"How did you get here?" Crystal asked looking over at Brant.

"Some small golden orb-looking thing," he answered. Crystal's eyes got big and shot her head back at Selene who nodded yes. She looked around at the group as they all had a serious look on their face, then Crystal knew this wasn't some practical joke.

"Come on, my father's this way," she said as she turned toward the stairs.

"All right, we're in," Kit said as she started to follow.

"Why are you surprised we've done this before?" Alpha asked as he walked next to her.

"She was just making a simple observation," Solar said as he followed behind as Selene watched everyone pass her.

"I don't need your outlook right now," Alpha replied as Brant walked up to Selene.

"So, what's all this about?" Brant asked knowing something was up.

"I don't completely understand it myself," Selene answered as the two walked side by side heading up the bamboo stairs. "But I have a feeling we're both about to find out," she added as they headed toward the large structure sitting higher than any other building in the valley.

26

Brant looked up the set of stairs that led up to a large bamboo structure. He looked up to see three balconies from each floor that rose out from the side of the building giving a view of the valley. Brant stepped up to Selene and Crystal as they made their way up.

"So, squirrel girl," he said with a grin getting their attention. "You're a princess?" Crystal looked at Selene with one eyebrow raised impressed how Brant wasn't afraid to ask whatever was on his mind.

"No, I'm the daughter of the chief," Crystal explained.

"Same difference," Brant replied as they walked up to a deck with a small door divided by a dark green curtain acting as the main entrance. They stopped walking as they stood next to the door waiting for everyone to catch up.

"You know the drill," Crystal said looking at everyone. "So, if there is anything you need to get off your chest now's the chance," she said. Brant looked around at the group wondering what this all meant. He looked at Alpha, Kit, and Solar who were looking back at Crystal but, when he looked over at Selene, she was looking at the ground. "Selene?" Crystal asked seeing her do the same thing. Selene looked up and nodded her head yes but the look in her eyes told a different story, but Crystal had to accept that answer. "Okay, let's go," she said turning to the curtain but stopping before she moved the green divider.

"You're going in last," she said looking at Brant. "So, tie your shoe or something."

"Okay," Brant said in a that-was-weird sort of tone. Selene looked at Brant with a look of worry in her eyes. He looked back wondering what was bothering her but Crystal walked in forcing the party in the same direction as Brant bent down to untie his shoe and started to tie it again.

"Hey, Daddy," Crystal said walking in. Everyone followed in the room. It wasn't a huge room but big enough to hold events, and the floor was made of bamboo like the rest of the village. The ceilings were high with stairs on both sides of the room that led up to the other levels, and at the center of the main hall was a firepit. "I brought some friends," she said walking to the other side of the room where an old man with white hair, a beard, and gray eyes sat on a bamboo seat.

"Young Selene," he said as everyone walked up to the throne.

"Chief," Selene said with a small bow.

"I was wondering when you'd get here," the chief said while Crystal stood next to her father.

"I told you he was expecting us," Alpha whispered up to Kit.

"There's the sarcastic remark I was waiting for," the chief said but he never made eye contact with anyone, he just looked at the floor, then over at the wall, or ceiling for a moment then back to the floor.

"I didn't want to disappoint you, sir," Alpha said with a grin. The chief laughed as the wind blew through holes in both walls.

"So, why are you here?" The chief asked.

"We need your help," Selene answered.

"Oh, I know that, otherwise you wouldn't be here," he said back with a grin. Suddenly Brant walked moving the green curtain and making his way into the room. The chief straightened up and looked toward the door as Brant walked looking around at the structure around him. "Crystal, who is that?" He asked in a soft voice.

"A human named Brant," she answered. The chief looked over in Brant's direction with a surprised look across his face as he walked up with the others.

"Took you long enough," Solar said with a grin.

"I started to tie my shoe, but I accidentally put a knot in it so I had to undo that and retie my shoe for a third time," Brant explained.

"Cause that's such a hard endeavor to put yourself through," Kit replied with a smile.

"I know right," Brant said with a grin. He looked ahead to see the white-haired old man who looked like the same type of creature as Crystal looking at him with an intense look. Brant looked behind him to see if there was anything else he could be gazing at, but there wasn't anything. He turned around to see the old man still looking at him with his gray eyes. "Selene," he said, taking one step to the left.

"Yeah," she said as he stood next to her.

"Why is he looking at me like that?" Brant asked.

"He's blind," Selene answered.

"He is?" Brant asked. "We watched me take a step toward you," he said looking at the old creature.

"So?" She asked.

"He's looking right at me," Brant said, never taking his eyes off him, then he looked over at Selene. "Now, he's looking at you," he said looking at Selene. She looked down at the ground again, now Brant knew something was bothering her.

"Daddy?" Crystal asked, getting his attention. The old man blinked a few times as if he was lost in a daze and Crystal pulled him out of it. He reached up and grabbed Crystal's shoulder as he took a deep breath while everyone watched. "What's wrong?" She asked

"Go ahead and introduce him to me," he answered rubbing his hand on his beard. Crystal looked at her father with a worried look then over at Brant.

"Brant Wilson, this is my father Oath, chief of the Valley of Light," Crystal introduced. "Daddy, this is Brant," she said looking at Oath.

"Nice to meet you," Brant said as he tried to figure out what was happening.

"When Eclipse attacked our homes, we thought he would come for us, but he never did," Oath explained as everyone listened. "But I was able to see we would be safe for the time being."

"Wait—" Brant interrupted. "I thought you were blind?" He asked.

"Physically," Oath answered. "But the light allows me to see things differently."

"You're a Protector?" Brant asked.

"No," he answered. "I'm unable to wield it like Selene and the others, but I can see a person's past, and future."

"That's not creepy at all," Brant said looking at Oath.

"You get used to it," Kit chimed as everyone stood in the quiet room.

"Like I'm going to believe that," Brant said not buying it for a second.

"The golden rob?" Oath started. "That's why you're here, right?" He asked looking at Selene. She nodded yes.

"What is it?" Brant asked.

"It's known as a Reality Stabilizer," Oath started. "Long ago, at the time when the ancients of our world came to Reavella searching for a place to call home. When they arrived, they discovered a light that surrounded and flowed through the life of this peaceful world. They quickly discovered that they, too, had the light of Reavella; they all believed that just by stepping foot here they acquired the strange gift, but not everyone received it. Only a select few bestowed the honor of wielding it as if the light was hand-picking whom it wanted. With this great honor, they created the first legion of Protectors, and as the ancients multiplied so did the Protector's numbers," he explained as Brant listened. "One day they decided to create a series of devices to help contain the dark forces for those who didn't have that ability and with that they created the Reality Stabilizer."

"What does it do?" Brant asked as he started to get the answers he searched for.

"The ancients believed that their world was one of many so they created a device to contain them and keep everything in balance," Oath continued. "Everything was going great when the worst happened."

"Eclipse?" Brant asked.

"Yes," Oath answered. "He arrived one day with forces too great to count. He attacked Reavella and the Protectors fought against the dark lord. After he conquered our world, he hunted down the rest of the Protectors, but that part you know," he explained. "About seven years ago, Eclipse found the Reality Stabilizer and tried to unleash its power and take over all of reality."

"What happened?" Brant asked.

"All the Protectors that were in hiding came out and stopped Eclipse, but the only ones who survived were Selene and the others around you," he answered. Brant looked over at Selene who looked back down at the ground.

"Really?" He asked impressed.

"Yes," Oath answered before she could. "No one knows Eclipse more than she does," Brant looked over at Selene with a smile thinking that was pretty cool.

"Are you a stalker?" He asked with a chuckle.

"You don't know," Crystal said as her eyes got big.

"Know what?" Brant asked looking at Crystal who looked at Selene. He looked over at Selene who couldn't look Brant in the eye, then he looked at the others who had a worried look across their face. "What? What don't I know?" He asked looking at Oath.

"Selene is the daughter of Eclipse," Oath answered. Brant took a step back in amazement.

"He's kidding, right?" Brant asked looking at Selene. She looked up at him with her eyes watery giving Brant his answer. "It's the truth?" He asked amazed. "Why didn't you tell me?"

"How could I?" Selene said trying to defend herself.

"Pretty easily, actually," Brant said back. "Is there anything else she's not telling me?" He asked Oath.

"No," he answered. "She and her sister Darcy arrived in Reavella when they were young."

"She's your sister," Brant said with a chuckle of disbelief shaking his head. "Did you know?" He asked looking over at Alpha and the others.

"We knew," Alpha answered.

"You all knew, and you didn't tell me?" Brant asked.

"It wasn't for us to say," Kit replied.

"No, but you could all have at least told me back at The Hidden," Brant snapped back. "Your father was killed by Eclipse," he said remembering what she told him. "And I fell for it."

"Brant, please," Selene said looking at Brant with her eyes still watery.

"Would you have come along if she had told you everything?" Solar asked.

"Yes," Brant answered without hesitating. "Then, I would have known you were telling me the truth and wanted to help me."

"But we did," Selene replied. "There's something you haven't told us, and it's written all over your face," she said making Oath straighten up again.

"Yes, but I'm the daughter of an apparent cold-blooded killer," Brant replied.

"I'm not like my father," Selene said looking at Brant as everyone just watched.

"I'm sorry, Selene," Brant said. "I did trust you because I thought you would be different from everybody else," he said turning back to Oath. Selene looked down at the ground as her eyes got watery again. "I just want to get home."

"Well, that's the problem," Oath started. "Since you were the one who opened it the first time, only you can open it again."

"That's why Eclipse wants me," Brant said adding the pieces together.

"The only way to get it back is by stopping Eclipse with the group that surrounds you," Oath explained.

"I'm sorry, did you not hear the conversation he just had?" Brant asked reaching the end of his rope. "Why on earth would I trust them enough to go home?"

"Because if you don't, all of reality will be lost," Oath answered. "Eclipse blames the Protectors for what happened, and he will stop at nothing to conquer what he thinks is rightfully his," he explained. Brant looked over his shoulder where everyone stood, then back at Oath.

"Fine," he said biting his lip. "But only because I don't have a choice," Brant said.

"I'd advise staying here for the night," Oath said.

"Sounds good," Selene said looking at the group. Brant started to walk toward the door looking at Selene as he walked by, but Oath wasn't done.

"What about your mother?" He asked. Brant stopped cold as everyone watched him.

"Both of my parents left me at the orphanage," Brant answered not turning around.

"That's what you like to think," Oath replied making Brant turn.

"Don't play mind games with me, old man," Brant said reaching his limit.

"The only mind game you're playing is your own," Oath snapped back. "I can see you in a hospital room with her lying in a bed," Oath started as everyone watched Brant.

"That's enough," Brant said but Oath kept going.

"She was dying from cancer and all you could do was watch as she cried in pain," he continued.

"Enough," Brant said looking at the floor and fighting back his memories.

"It was raining outside as she held your hand," Oath told as everyone watched Brant.

"Enough," Brant said as his eyes got watery. "Enough."

"The next moment your mother told you she loved you as she took her last breath," Oath finished, but Brant couldn't take it anymore.

"Enough!" He shouted. Everyone looked back at Brant as he stood there in the quiet. He looked up at Oath with his nose red and eyes watery. He looked over at Selene with her ears back as she looked at Brant with a sorry look in her eyes.

"And not far after that your father ran away with another woman and left you alone," Oath said as everyone looked at

Brant as he stared at the floor. "Sounds like you and Selene aren't that different after all," he finished, and then the room stood in silence as they looked at Brant. Brant wanted to come back at the old creature but, with everything fresh in his mind, he couldn't come up with anything. He simply turned around and walked out of the building as Selene started to follow, but she was stopped.

"Better give him some space," Oath interjected. Selene stopped and watched Brant move the curtain and leave as the sun started to set.

27

T HE THREE MOONS OF Reavella started to rise, peeking their heads over the rocked valley. The people of the valley started to gather at the Great Hall as everyone made their way into the bamboo structure. Brant walked into the now crowded hall to see the firepit at the center burning, lighting up the room. He looked around as all the people lined up by a long table on the far-right wall where food was being served. He walked over to the line and waited. Brant leaned out and looked ahead of the line to see the group he traveled with getting their food. He leaned back before they could see him as he walked up to the table. Brant looked at the food that was being served, but none of it looked like the food where he was from. The first tray had what looked like a burger; if the burgers from Earth looked blue with green buns. Brant grabbed the burger-like food and went to find a seat since he wasn't that hungry. He looked to the left side of the firepit to see Selene and the gang sitting. Brant walked by as they watched him make his way to the other side of the fire. On the ground surrounding the firepit were small pillows so the guest didn't have to sit on the hard bamboo. Brant sat down with a pillow open to his right but all the other seats were taken around him. He reached down, grabbed his food, took a bite, and to his surprise, it tasted pretty good. As Brant ate his food Selene watched him from across the room.

"Talk to him," Kit said as they sat around.

"He doesn't want to talk," she replied.

"I think he will," Kit said looking at Selene.

"He thinks I lied to him and, in a way, I did," Selene retaliated.

"Yeah, but I don't think that's what's bothering him," Kit said looking at Brant.

"Of course, it is," Selene said thinking Kit missed the whole point of their conversation. "I should've told him everything when we first met him, but I didn't and now he doesn't want our help. All because I lied to him," she said getting frustrated with herself.

"No, that's not it," Kit said. "Look at his eyes," Selene looked over at Brant looking down at his plate not making eye contact with anyone. "Look at him closely, he's not mad," Kit explained. Selene looked at Brant as the fire lit up the room. "He's afraid," she said looking over Brant. "What Oath said about his mother got him, even more than Eclipse being your father," Kit said adding the pieces together. Selene looked at Brant through the fire's tips to see Brant with a look of fear in his eyes she didn't notice till Kit pointed it out.

"But why didn't he tell us?" Selene asked. "He complained I never told him about my father, but he never told us about his mother," she said still looking at Brant.

"For the same reason," Kit answered. "You both were protecting yourself from your past," Kit said looking back at Selene. She looked at Brant as he finished eating with her ears back wanting to go and talk to him but she didn't know where to start. Selene watched Brant as Crystal walked up to Brant and sat down by him.

"Mind if I join you?" She asked as she started to sit down not waiting for permission.

"What do you want, princess?" Brant asked not in a mood to talk.

"Again, I'm not a princess," Crystal answered now sitting by Brant. She was waiting for a comeback but one never came. She looked at Brant who was still looking at the floor. "Sorry about my father's abruptness. He can see what most can't, but his delivery can be tough sometimes," Crystal apologized.

"Some things should be left unsaid," Brant said still looking at the ground.

"The longer something goes unsaid the worse it gets," Crystal said looking at Brant. "Why would you torture your mind like that?" She asked.

"It's complicated," he answered.

"I don't think it's as complicated as you make it out to be," Crystal replied. Just before any of them got in another word Oath stood up and raised his hand getting the attention of the people. They all directed their attention to the chief filling the balconies of the levels above as it grew quiet.

"Citizens of the Valley," Oath started as everyone looked over at him. "We are honored to have with us tonight the last Protectors of Reavella," he said motioning to Selene and the others but not Brant, but he was okay with it. "Go ahead, guys, stand up so everyone can see you," Oath said with a grin. They all looked at each other and stood up as everyone started to clap looking at the group, but Brant didn't stand.

"I hate it when everyone looks at us," Solar said as they looked around the room.

"You're in the wrong profession if you have that going for you," Alpha replied with a grin.

"But we have another member that I must introduce," Oath started. "Tonight, we are honored to have a new member whom the light has chosen," he said as Brant heard the crowd whisper; he knew where he was going with it, but Brant couldn't leave without drawing attention to himself. "And he may be the key to our victory over the dark king. Brant Wilson everyone," Oath said gesturing his hand at Brant. Everyone looked in that direction but Brant didn't stand up.

"Stand up," Crystal whispered at Brant.

"I can't move my feet," he said seeing everyone look over at him.

"Come on," Crystal said grabbing his arm and standing up. Brant followed Crystal up so she wouldn't pull on him in front of everyone.

"What is that?" He heard someone ask as the crowd whispered looking at Brant.

"Brant is the first human we've ever had the pleasure of hosting," Oath started. "He's from a world far from here and his homeland is full of strong and proud people, but Brant did not come here intentionally. He has brought with him a Reality Stabilizer," Oath said, and as soon as he did the crowd whispered louder. "Now, now," Oath said regaining the attention of the people. "If one of us went to his world we'd be out of our element as much as he is now," he said, defending Brant as everyone listened. "But if you would talk to Brant, he would let you believe he is not that special. You see, he's had a hard life and believes he does not deserve a second chance," Oath explained. Selene shot her head over at Brant as Oath continued.

"He thinks his shot of redemption is gone, but do we believe in this human?" Oath asked. "Do you have the faith in him to save us all from the darkness?" The crowd started to clap and cheer as if Oath's stamp of approval was enough for them. Brant looked around taken aback by the cheers from strangers. He looked over at Selene, Kit, Alpha, and Solar to see them clapping as they looked back at him with a smile across their faces. "But," Oath said as it started to grow quiet again. "You may ask yourself why would he do this? Why would he want to help us when so many of those he'd tried to help pulled him down?" Oath asked the crowd as Brant looked up at the old creature. "Well, the answer may be simpler than what you think," he said, then he looked at Brant. "It's what his mother would want him to do," Oath said looking at Brant in the eye with a gentle smile on his face. Brant looked down at the ground as Oath continued. "Things may get dark but let us celebrate in the light," Oath said as he sat down and the crowd started to talk and laugh like they did before. Brant took a deep breath as he stared at the ground. He turned toward the door and started to walk out as Selene watched and followed him out. Alpha started to follow but Kit grabbed his shoulder.

"Best we leave this to just the two of them," Kit explained as they watched Brant walk out and Selene followed not far behind.

28

SELENE MOVED THE CURTAIN divider and looked to her right to see Brant leaning on the railing of the platform they were standing on. She walked over and leaned on the fence right next to him as he looked down at the water below.

"Hey," Selene said trying to get a conversation going.

"Hey," Brant replied still looking down.

"Listen about what happened," Selene started. "I should've told you everything from the start. I never meant to lie to you, and I'm sorry I did," she apologized. Brant looked up and over at Selene as Reavella's moons hung high.

"It's okay," Brant said with a soft grin. "I guess we both have memories we can't quite touch," he said, then they stood in silence for a moment or two as the sound of moving water filled the dead noise.

"Sorry about your mom. She sounds like she was quite a person," she said looking at Brant again. Brant looked down at the water and took a deep breath before he looked back up at Selene.

"She was," Brant said looking at the stars above. "When we would drive in the car or just bored at the house, she would turn music on and we would dance and all our problems would seem to vanish," he said with a soft smile remembering all the times he had with his mom.

"So that's where your love for music comes from," Selene replied.

"Yes," Brant said, remembering all the memories he had with her. "She loved blaring it so everyone could hear," he recalled with a smile.

"How many songs did you listen to?" Selene asked as they leaned on the railing. Brant reached into his pocket, pulled his phone out, opened his playlist, and handed it to Selene. "Wow!" she said scrolling through all the options. "You have over three hundred and fifty songs on this thing?!" She asked a little surprised.

"Yeah, it's excessive," Brant joked making Selene laugh. "But it was fun because every time we would listen together, we always got a different selection," Selene just kept scrolling looking at every option like a song called *Billboards on Sunset* by Sarah Reeves and *The Prodigal* by Josiah Queen.

"Which one was your favorite?" Selene asked still scrolling.

"Scroll back up to the top," he answered. Brant reached into his pocket and pulled out his EarPods just as Selene scrolled to the top of the playlist.

"What are those?" She asked.

"You listen through them," Brant answered with a grin. He opened the white case and placed the right earbud in his ear, then he grabbed the left earbud and gently placed it in Selene's ear.

"Cool," Selene said looking at Brant as he grabbed his phone. Brant smiled and selected the top song called *Tonight* by FM Static. Selene's eyes got big and her ears raised for a moment as a guitar started playing and a voice started singing.

"I remember the times we spent together. All those drives, we had a million questions all about our lives. And when we got to New York

everything felt right. I wish you were here with me, tonight," he sang as Selene listened and leaned against the railing.

"The melody is pleasant!" She shouted with the music still playing in her ear, making him laugh. Brant took a deep breath and looked up at the stars just as the lead singer sang louder along with the instruments as the chorus started to play.

"Tonight, I've fallen and I can't get up. I need your loving hands to come and pick me up. And every night I miss you I can just look up and know the stars are holding you, holding you, holding you tonight," the song played while Brant looked up at the stars as the music continued. *"I remember about the time you told me when you were eight. All those things you said that night that just couldn't wait. I remember the car you were last seen in and the games we would play. All the times we spilled our coffees and stayed out way too late. I remember the time you sat and told me about your Jesus and how not to look back even if no one believes us. When it hurts so bad, sometimes not having you here,"* Selene looked at Brant with his eyes a little watery.

"Tonight, I've fallen and I can't get up. I need your loving hands to come and pick me up. And every night I miss you I can just look up and know the stars are holding you, holding you, holding you tonight," the song finished and the music faded as Selene looked over at Brant who wiped his nose for a second.

"That was beautiful," Selene said breaking the silence.

"It was one of my mom's favorite songs. Every time it plays, I think of her," he explained, then he placed the EarPods back in their case and slid them and his phone back into his pocket.

"Sorry you lost her the way you did," Selene said as they stood by the railing with the water flowing underneath.

"Thanks," he said. "My mom was my best friend. She loved music and shared her favorites with me along with new music. She even left some voice recordings before she died, but I never could bring myself to listen to them. I was never close with my dad but I still loved him. When my mom died he wanted to start a new life, and he threw me out like a piece of trash," Brant said looking at the water again. "Can't say I blame him. I tried to prove I was worth having but I guess he saw me as irredeemable," he explained but stopped to take another deep breath remembering everything as clear as day. "I guess he was right," Brant said. Selene watched as Brant took another deep breath while looking down at the water.

"When I arrived with my father, he discovered I had the light before I did. I was so young I had no idea what he was doing," Selene started, making Brant look at her. "He used me as a tool to hunt down the Protectors. I slaughtered them, everyone I could to make my father proud of me," she said biting her lip for a second, but continued. "But when I saw what my father wanted to do with the Reality Stabilizer I couldn't just stand by and watch. I betrayed my father and helped the Protectors but I lost my family and my home," Selene explained. "Still think you're the only irredeemable monster in the universe?" She asked.

"I wouldn't view you as a monster," Brant said with a smile. "Maybe rough around the edges, and a tad cocky but still," he joked. Selene smiled as she looked out over the village.

"Really?" She asked looking back at Brant with a smile. "We were having a moment and you had to go and ruin it," Selene said with a smile.

"Just trying to lighten the mood," Brant replied, then he looked down at his hand. "Do you have an instruction manual for how this light works?" He asked. "I mean I love the mystery and all, but I would love to know how to use it."

"There are no instructions to learn," Selene answered. "Just imagine and feel what you want the light to do, and believe it will happen," she explained. Brant looked down at his hand, then he held it up with the palm of his hand up toward the starry sky. He thought about his hand lighting up yellow like the others and, just as if he hit a switch, his hand lit up. Then he thought about a small ball hovering over his palm and no sooner than he did a gold ball rose from his hand. It started small like a marble but by the time it floated a few inches away from his hand, it became the size of a baseball. "There you go," Selene said as she watched with a smile. Brant looked over as Selene watched the yellow ball. Brant threw the ball up and away from the Great Hall and the yellow ball exploded like a small firecracker lighting up a small area yellow for a brief moment. "Good job," Selene said with a smile.

"Thanks," Brant said as he watched the light fade from his hands. "Still feels weird having abilities like this."

"Don't worry, you'll get used to it," Selene reassured.

"Well, it helps being surrounded by remarkable creatures like you," Brant said with a soft smile. Selene looked back at Brant with the same smile as the water flowed. They stood there for a moment or two, and then out of nowhere Selene cried out in pain.

"Ah!" She yelled leaning against the railing.

"What's wrong?" Brant asked not knowing what to do or where she was hurting. Selene looked up and out into the village as she took a deep breath. Brant gently grabbed her shoulder and helped her to her feet.

"He's here," she said getting to her feet.

"Who?" Brant asked, not feeling anything.

"My father," Selene answered, looking at Brant with fear in her eyes.

"**S**TAY HERE," SELENE SAID as she ran back inside the Great Hall just as Oath started to address the crowd again. Brant watched her run inside, then he turned around to look over the valley. It looked empty, and there wasn't any sound that warranted a panic. Selene ran back outside but this time she wasn't alone as everyone followed.

"What's going on?" Kit asked as they stood on the bamboo deck.

"Eclipse is here," Selene answered as she watched the village as it stood in silence.

"Are you sure?" Alpha asked, but Selene just watched the village looking for any sign of movement but still found nothing.

"Did you see anything?" Solar asked Brant.

"No," Brant said looking out at the village, then back at everyone. "Nothing's happened."

"I don't like it," Kit added as everyone looked for Eclipse or one of his soldiers. They all looked around from the village rooftops to the water below but nothing was there. Alpha looked out onto the village when he heard a faint rock sound. His right ear twitched when he heard a small pebble fell. He looked at the top of the cannon to see a shadowy figure with a beak moving.

"There," he said getting everyone's attention. They looked at Alpha who was looking up which made them do the same. Brant looked up and saw the figure moving around followed by a handful of other shadowy figures. Kit looked at the other cannon walls to see more troops on top.

"They're boxing us in," she said looking around the cliff tops to see more figures.

"What do we do?" Solar asked. Selene looked out into the village trying to come up with a plan but all she thought about was her father's presence. "Selene," he said again getting her attention.

"I . . . ," she started but couldn't think of anything. "We can try to get back to the ship," Selene said, saying the first semidecent idea that came to mind.

"How are we going to get there when we're surrounded by ravens and Eclipse?" Alpha asked.

"Do you have any better ideas?" Selene questioned back getting more and more stressed. Brant looked out over the railing and into the village. He felt like he was hearing the sound of footsteps, but they were far off. He looked out tilting his head as if he could hear not only the footsteps but where they were going.

"Eclipse is on the left side of the valley, and he's heading toward a small hub at the center of the village," Brant said still looking at the village. Everyone looked at each other with a curious look across their face.

"How do you know that?" Kit asked.

"I . . . I don't know," Brant answered. "But I know he's over there," Kit looked over at Selene with her eyebrows raised.

"We'll have to go with it," Selene said running out of options and time. "We'll sneak along the right side of the valley and make our way back to the ship," she explained.

"Are you serious?" Alpha questioned, amazed. "Okay," he said just accepting the plan.

"Wait? We're going to run away?" Brant asked.

"Look, if it was anyone else, I'd say we stand and fight; but, it's Eclipse," Selene answered.

"So?" Brant questioned back still missing the point. "This guy wants me and I'd like to introduce myself," he said wanting to meet the man who was hunting him down.

"This guy's a lunatic, a psycho. He'll kill you without thinking twice," Selene answered. "We're getting out of the village, and we'll figure out where to go from there."

"But we have him outnumbered," Brant added.

"We're getting out of the valley," Selene said as she started to make her way toward the stairs. "End of discussion," she said making her way down the stairs. Brant watched her run down the stairs followed by Kit and Alpha, but Solar stopped by Brant.

"Don't worry, this is for the best," Solar reassured before he ran down the stairs. Brant watched them run down. He bit his lip in frustration but what more could he do? Brant ran down the stairs and followed the group as they ran to the right. Brant ran behind them as they weaved around the pathways gradually making their way through.

"Keep on the lookout just in case one of the ravens decides to get an itchy trigger finger," Selene said as they ran.

"I don't like it. They can see us running and they aren't doing a thing about it," Kit replied looking up at the cliff tops.

"Once we get out it won't matter," Selene said.

"You mean if we get out," Alpha corrected.

"Thanks, Alpha," Selene said with a smirk. "I feel better about the situation already," she said as they ran. They ran through the valley passing home after home. Brant started to slow down as everyone ran farther ahead. He watched them round another corner as he stopped, and then he took off toward the left side of the valley.

3 0

BRANT STARTED TO WALK down the bamboo pathway looking around for anything that looked like Eclipse. He didn't even know what Eclipse looked like, but he was hoping he'd know just by looking at him. Brant walked over to a small courtyard at the center of the valley. It was a circle and a fountain stood at the center of the platform that spouted the bright, crystal-blue water from below where small bamboo houses surrounded the courtyard. He walked into the courtyard and stood by the fountain as he looked around for the man everyone had been talking about. Brant looked around at the small pathways in front of him that led farther into the village but they were empty. Brant started to take a step to his right making his way around the fountain when the hairs on the back of his neck stood up and his arms got goosebumps. Brant looked behind him as he walked around the fountain. He looked around the fountain and down the pathway right behind him to see someone standing there just watching him. Brant looked over to see a figure with gray skin, a black robe, hair that was sticking up, and cold gray eyes. Brant stopped cold when his eyes met the stranger's eyes as he took a few steps toward Brant entering the courtyard.

"The boy I've heard so much about," Eclipse said looking at Brant. Brant just looked at Eclipse taken aback by the moment. For a tyrant, he had a presence, even his voice was impressive and yet oddly comforting. "At first I didn't know if the rumor was true but now that I get to have a good look at you, you are without a doubt a human."

"And you must be Eclipse," Brant said, managing to get it out.

"I'm glad I came out to meet you in person," Eclipse said as everything around them stood in silence.

"At least I wasn't able to disappoint you," Brant said trying to hide the fact he was intimidated. "So, what do you want?" He asked already knowing the answer but, he wanted to see what he had to say.

"It would seem I need your help," Eclipse answered.

"You don't say," Brant said sarcastically already knowing where he was going with this.

"Yes," Eclipse said playing along. "How would you like to join my army of fighters, and bring peace for all time?" He offered.

"And how would we be doing that?" Brant asked fishing for information.

"Through strength," Eclipse answered, but Brant knew the truth.

"Or you need me to open the Reality Stabilizer so you can conquer everything your heart desires," Brant said explaining everything for Eclipse. Eclipse smiled at Brant.

"Clever boy," he said with a small chuckle.

"Sorry, but I'm not interested," Brant said feeling more confident.

"You should reconsider," Eclipse started. "You can have everything you ever wanted."

"I never did like being bribed," Brant replied with a grin.

"Oh," Eclipse said with a smile. "It pains you, doesn't it? The only way you can get home is with the Reality Stabilizer, but I have it. So, the only way you can get home is through me," he said with a grin. Brant took a deep breath. He knew that, but now that Eclipse was standing in front of him it became more of a realization.

"I'm going home," Brant said gritting his teeth.

"Not as long as I have the Stabilizer," Eclipse retaliated. "And the only way you can have it is if you stop me."

"Why can't you just hand it over?" He asked. "It would be so much easier."

"I wanted to do this together, but I see that is out of the question," Eclipse said.

"Why on earth would I help you?" Brant asked. "You're a killer," Eclipse looked at Brant with a grin.

"That may be true, but you don't know the full story," he said. Brant looked at him wondering what he meant. "It's true, I slaughtered thousands of Protectors, but what chance do you think you have against me?"

"Sorry, old man, I just want to go home," Brant replied with a smirk.

"You have no idea of the power that is within reach," Eclipse said, getting agitated by Brant's cocky attitude.

"How long of a reach?" Brant joked.

"You're confusing confidence for intelligence," Eclipse said annoyed.

"At least I have what some people lack," he replied as the tension started to mount.

"Then you are a fool," Eclipse said taking a step toward Brant.

"That's not a new one. Can you come up with something original?" Brant asked with a grin. Eclipse tightened his fist with his arm down and a dark gray ball appeared as if formed like sand. He swung it up at Brant hitting him in the stomach and making him fly backwards.

31

B RANT FLEW BACK AND hit a small bamboo home crashing through the wall and into the house. Brant lay on the ground catching his breath.

"Okay," Brant said as he lay on the ground. He got up and jumped back through the hole he crashed through to see Eclipse slowly walking toward him. Brant raised his left hand and shot out a bright yellow beam at Eclipse. He leaned to the left just as the beam flew past his waist. Brant lowered his left and quickly raised his right hand and shot out another beam like he did before. The light flew through the air and sped toward Eclipse's head, but he leaned to his right just as it flew past the dark king.

"Is that all you have, my boy?" Eclipse asked as Brant saw a crate out of the corner of his eye.

"I'm learning," he answered, then he reached his hand out at the crate causing it to light up the air around it a bright yellow. Brant threw his arm in the direction he wanted it to go. The crate flew through the air toward Eclipse. He reached his hand out and stopped the crate making it float by his head with a black sand particle surrounding the crate and stopping it just before impact and letting it fall to the ground with a large bang.

"I think not," Eclipse said with a grin as reached his hand out at Brant. Suddenly, black sand appeared as it hurled toward Brant. Brant reached his hand out and created a shield as he did back at The Hidden. The dark sand sped through the air hitting Brant's shield, but unlike before, it crashed through the barrier, hitting Brant and sending him back hitting another wall of a bamboo house. He got to his knees and looked up at Eclipse taken aback by the fact he broke his shield with such ease.

"That was impressive, I'll give you that," Brant said getting to his feet.

"You have no idea what you're up against," Eclipse added.

"True, but I like a good mystery," Brant replied with a smirk. Eclipse gritted his teeth as Brant started to run toward him. Eclipse raised his hand so his fingers pointed up toward the sky, then the ground below Brant's feet gave way as a pillar of dark sand crashed through and upward sending Brant in the same direction. "Whoa!" Brant yelled as he flew up in the air. Eclipse reached his hand up and a dark pillar of sand appeared reaching up at Brant. Eclipse closed his fist and the sand rapped around Brant's ankle. Then he yanked his arm down at the ground, and just like it was obeying a command the sand followed Eclipse's motion and it threw Brant toward the ground. Brant slammed into the bamboo walkway causing it to crack and break. He tried to move but it was hard to get up. Even with the light, Eclipse was hitting him so hard it didn't matter too much. Eclipse watched Brant squirm as he reached into his pocket and pulled out a small, flat disk.

"Darcy, find the elder and bring him to me," he ordered.

"What about Selene?" Darcy questioned back.

"If she's here, she'll deliver herself to us. For now, find the leader of this pathetic town and bring him to me," Eclipse answered.

"Yes, Father," Darcy replied. Eclipse shut off the device and slid it back into his pocket as Brant managed to get to his feet. Eclipse looked over at Brant as he stood breathing hard and smiled knowing Brant couldn't touch him. Brant threw his hand out but Eclipse was ready and threw his hand at Brant before he could and hit Brant hard on the side sending him to the ground and creating another loud bang as Selene and the others ran through the village.

"What was that?" Selene asked as she stopped with the rocked archway just in front of them. She turned around and looked at the group but realized something wasn't right. "Wait, where's Brant?" She asked.

"Brant, he's right—" Alpha started as he turned around to look for him but he wasn't there. "Where is he?" He asked.

"Solar, he was right behind you, where is he?" Kit asked.

"I don't know, I don't have eyes in the back of my head," he answered.

"This is no time to joke around," Alpha replied.

"I wasn't joking, I don't have eyes in the back of my head," Solar said as if it was a new fun fact about him.

"Guys, seriously," Kit said breaking up the two. "Where is he?" She asked, then, suddenly, there was another crash.

"Oh, no," Selene said, dropping her ears back knowing where Brant snuck off to. Everyone's eyes turned to the village knowing at the same moment as Selene. "Let's go," Selene said as she started to run but Kit grabbed her arm.

"Selene," she said making her stop. "Eclipse will be waiting."

"So?" Selene asked turning around.

"You know more than anyone," Kit started. "He'll be waiting for us. The best way we can save Brant is by coming at Eclipse in a way he's not expecting," she explained. Selene looked into the village, then back at everyone else.

"Okay," she admitted. "Get to the ship," she ordered. They took off underneath the archway and down the narrow pathway leading back to the ship as another crash filled the area. Brant hit the side of another house as Eclipse fought Brant, but it was a one-sided match. He got on his feet and started to run at Eclipse but he was no match for him. Eclipse swung his hand toward him. Brant flew through the air just as Eclipse took a step to the side passing the dark king. Brant hit the railing causing it to crack and even snap in some places. Brant grit his teeth and started to get up as Eclipse walked up to him. Suddenly, Brant heard a sound he was familiar with. He looked up in time to see the ship he traveled in with everyone take off and sped off into the clouds. Brant's eyes got big as he watched the ship disappear.

"They left you," Eclipse said not expecting that outcome. "I thought she would come back for you," he said as Brant watched the sky. While Brant's back was turned Eclipse reached his hand out and threw it at Brant's hands. The black sand hit Brant's left wrist then his right forming handcuffs.

"Hey!" He shouted trying to break free but it was too late. Eclipse waved his hand back toward him sending Brant in the same direction as he flew back hitting the base of the fountain.

"You should have taken my offer when you had the chance," Eclipse said with a grin as Brant leaned back against the fountain.

32

SECONDS PASSED AND THE small courtyard filled with ravens with their dark purple armor scattered around securing the area. Two guards pulled Brant up on his feet and started to walk him over to Eclipse who moved in front of the fountain facing in the same direction as the Grand Hall. The guards walked Brant over in front of Eclipse who took a step forward so Brant's back was facing the fountain and hit him in the back of the legs making him fall to his knees.

"Thanks for being so gentle with me," Brant said sarcastically. He looked up at Eclipse who just glared down at Brant with a look of frustration across his face, but Brant didn't understand why. He beat him pretty easily so what was his deal? Before he could say a word, they heard the sound of footsteps behind them. Eclipse turned around and Brant looked ahead to see Darcy escorting Oath and another guard who was escorting Crystal. Darcy walked Oath up a few feet in front of Eclipse and hit him in the leg making him kneel just like Brant, but they took Crystal to the side.

"The old man knew we were coming. Everyone was gone except for these two rodents," Darcy explained.

"The citizens were not the target," Eclipse replied looking down at Oath. At first, Oath wouldn't make eye contact with Eclipse but as he stepped up to the old man he looked up and into the dark king's eyes. "I know who you are," Eclipse said trying to get into Oath's head.

"I know where you come from. Before you conquered Reavella and slaughtered our people," Oath retaliated.

"Mind games won't get you anywhere," Eclipse said looking down at the old man.

"The times for games are over," Oath started. "Soon everything you have built will be destroyed, and the darkness will be underneath's lights heel."

"Really?" Eclipse asked. "And who will be the one to stop me?" He asked. Oath smiled and looked over at Brant.

"Him," he answered. Brant's eyes got big thinking Oath had lost his mind. Eclipse looked over at Brant with one eyebrow raised as he looked at Brant with a judgmental look.

"You must be blind," Eclipse replied looking back at Oath. "He did not touch me when we fought in your pathetic town. So, what do you see in this insignificant human?" He asked. "How is he going to do what thousands could not?"

"My eyes see more than yours ever will," Oath explained. "And I can see the end of the path you're on."

"What do you see?" Eclipse asked.

"I see your defeat, as worlds see the end of your rule and this boy will be left standing," Oath answered. Eclipse clenched his fist hard as he looked down at the old man. He opened his hand toward Oath causing a black ring to appear around his throat. Oath tried to gasp for air as Eclipse raised his hand raising Oath along with it till they were at eye level. Crystal watched as her father struggled and Brant watched in horror, afraid of what the dark king would do. Eclipse watched with a smirk as Oath struggled for air. Oath struggled for air with his eyes turning bloodshot red. "You . . . will . . . never . . . rule . . . reality," Oath managed to get out. Eclipse's smile went away and he tightened his fist stopping all air inside.

"Dad!" Crystal screamed as her father hung in the air lifeless. Eclipse turned around facing Brant as he watched in horror. He opened his hand and the chief fell to the ground just in front of Brant.

"Bring the human back to the palace," he ordered. The ravens grabbed Brant's arms and lifted him to his feet and started to escort him away from the scene. Eclipse started to follow as Darcy joined her father's side.

"What about her?" She asked looking at Crystal who hung her head and started to cry with no intent of stopping soon.

"Leave her, this is more effective than any cell we can put her in," he answered as he walked.

"But she'll contact Selene," Darcy replied. "They'll know what we've done."

"I am counting on it," Eclipse said with a grin.

33

ALL STOOD QUIET AS Crystal sat on a rock in front of the two waterfalls. She had her head buried in her legs as she thought about her father and the thought of him being gone. She sat alone with just the sound of falling water filling the area when, suddenly, a ship flew through the small tunnel and landed in front of her. She looked up in time to see the ramp extend down to the ground and the group of outlaws walked out.

"We got your distress signal," Selene said as they walked up to Crystal who just got to her feet. "What happened? Where's Oath?" She asked. Crystal looked at the ground, then back up at Selene with her eyes watery and nose red.

"He's gone," she answered trying to keep her composure.

"He's been captured?" Solar asked.

"No, he's gone!" Crystal yelled as she wiped her nose. Selene dropped her ears back as she looked at the others with the same stunned look across their faces. Selene looked back at Crystal as she continued to cry.

"Alpha, get her on the ship," Selene said looking at Crystal. Alpha walked up to Crystal and gently put his arm around her shoulders.

"Come on," he said gently leading her to the ship. "Can't guarantee it's clean, we weren't expecting company," Alpha joked trying to lighten the mood. Crystal smiled as she walked and the others watched her pass.

"Wait," Crystal said as she stopped and turned around to face everyone. "Eclipse has Brant."

"Where?" Selene asked.

"The palace," Crystal answered, then she turned back around and headed into the ship with Alpha right by her side. Selene took a deep breath as she looked at the ground thinking of what to do.

"What do we do?" Kit asked. Selene looked up at Kit, then started to walk to the ship. "This is going to be fun," Kit said with a grin knowing what that meant as she started to follow everyone inside the ship.

34

TWO RAVEN GUARDS GUIDED Brant down a light gray hallway with bright white lights down the center. There were silver doors on both sides, each about five or six feet from each other. Near the center of the hallway, the guards turned and a silver door opened. The guards escorted Brant into the room. He looked around at the windowless room with the same silver color spread throughout the circular room and a metal chair at the center. The ravens walked Brant up to the metal chair, forcefully turned him around, and pushed him up. Brant stepped back from the not-so-gentle push and metal clamps shot around by his arms, wrists, and ankles prohibiting him from moving. He looked down at the contraption he was in. When he first walked in he thought it was a chair of some sort but now that he was forced into it Brant realized he was standing up more than he was in a sitting position. The guards who escorted Brant in turned and stood at attention by the door. Brant looked down at the metal clamps around his arms and legs. He tried to move and break free but it was no use. While he tried to break free, he heard a voice from the doorway.

"I wouldn't try that if I were you," Brant looked up to see Darcy walking into the circular cell. "My father doesn't like it when Protectors try to make a getaway after he goes through the hard work of capturing them," Darcy said with a grin.

"I wouldn't dream of upsetting him," Brant replied. "After all he asked so nicely."

"You want my advice?" Darcy asked. "Just do what he says. It'll be better for everyone," she said answering her question.

"Will it be better for everyone? While people like Oath and I are slaughtered for standing up for what's right," Brant said never taking his eyes off of Darcy.

"My father just wants peace," Darcy replied.

"Through terror," Brant added. Darcy looked down at the silver floor for a moment but before she had a chance to look up they heard a new voice from behind.

"Peace through absolute order," they looked toward the door to see Eclipse standing in the doorway. "Terror will only come to those who resist," he said as he walked into the room.

"And that's okay with you?" Brant asked. "You can watch as thousands die all because they oppose you?"

"It's not so hard to do," Eclipse answered. Brant looked into the dark ruler's eyes to see he was dead serious. There was no remorse or guilt in his eyes; then, he knew he not only meant what he said but he also knew that he wasn't safe from Eclipse's wrath. "Now," he said moving the conversation onward. "You're going to open the Reality Stabilizer or—" he started but was interrupted.

"Or what?" Brant asked. "I know you need me to open it. So, as long as I refuse you can't touch me."

"I wanted to do this together but if you refuse, I'm afraid I will have to take further action," Eclipse replied as he walked up closer to Brant.

"Oh, no! How will you manage?" Brant asked sarcastically. Eclipse looked at Brant who just stared back at the dark figure.

"You're not afraid," Eclipse said mildly impressed.

"Why would I be?" Brant asked back with a smirk.

"You hide your feelings well but not enough," Eclipse said. "But your mind will speak or it will break," he said holding his hand up next to Brant's head.

"What are you doing?" Brant asked but, in a matter of a few seconds, he found out. Brant blinked hard as he felt Eclipse's power inside his mind slithering through like a snake. "Ah," he said gritting his teeth, trying to fight back.

"You lost your mother," Eclipse started. "Your father left you alone, so you became closed off from the outside world, refusing to talk to anyone."

"Get out of my head," Brant said trying to fight the darkness in his mind.

"But after all that happened you hoped to make at least one friend so you weren't alone in the world, but you still ended up short every time," Eclipse continued. "I would go through the names you've been called but we don't have that kind of time," he said with a smirk, enjoying going through Brant's memories. "At night when you're desperate to sleep you imagine you and your mother on a beach. But you found a friend in Selene and the others. Give them long enough they'll disappoint you, believe me."

"Get out of my head," Brant repeated trying to shut out Eclipse.

"All the information I need is in there, and now you're going tell me how to open the Reality Stabilizer," Eclipse said stretching his arm out straighter. Brant felt Eclipse move around faster in his mind. He leaned forward trying to shut out Eclipse while he looked in his gray eyes, but as he looked, he started to feel something. "It's okay I feel it, too," Eclipse said with his arm still out. Brant just focused on fighting Eclipse in his mind, but the more he fought he started to feel something new like a voice whispering in his mind. Eclipse started to get a look of worry or even fear in his eyes as Brant straightened up in his restraints.

"You," Brant started. "You're haunted," he said as Eclipse leaned forward as if he was fighting something no one could see. "Haunted by your wife's cry."

"Ah!" Eclipse yelled yanking his arm away from Brant. Brant felt Eclipse leave his mind but he still felt what Eclipse was hiding like a news anchor hearing the news through a source in their ear.

"That's why you came to Reavella," he started looking at the ground sorting through the information dump in his head. "Your wife was sick. You came here to see if the Protectors could heal her," Brant said as Eclipse looked at Brant with a look of fear and anger across his face. "They told you their abilities couldn't heal people, but you didn't believe them. When your wife died you blamed the Protectors. So, you want to make everything the way it was before you came to Reavella," Brant said, then he looked up at Eclipse. "You think if you conquer reality it will make everything better, bring her back somehow, and reunite yourself with Selene," he said looking at Eclipse who just looked at him with a look of shock. "Wait," Brant said as more information still came in. "Selene," he started. "Selene's not—" Brant started but was cut off.

"Enough!" He shouted, and then he stepped closer to Brant. "No one has ever resisted me before," Eclipse said walking back up to Brant. "Any hope you had of leaving is gone."

"I wasn't counting on it," Brant snapped back.

"You have no idea what I can do," Eclipse said trying to intimidate Brant.

"The only thing I know, I see, is you getting more and more frustrated," Brant said with a grin. Eclipse clenched his fist by his side looking at Brant with all the hatred he could have for anyone.

"Very well," Eclipse said taking a deep breath and releasing his fist. "Perhaps you can help me relieve some of my frustration," Eclipse looked over and nodded at Darcy who was standing by the wall with a small panel just to her right. She pressed a small red button and the three small metal arms extended downward with a small point facing Brant. Brant watched as they stopped on both sides of Brant and the third facing his back. Suddenly a bright green beam-like light shot out hitting Brant.

"Ah!" He yelled. It was a sharp agonizing pain. It felt like it was passing through the light that was supposed to protect him and cut through his body, putting pressure and pain in every spot, all the while Eclipse watched with a cold grin across his face.

"**A**H!" BRANT YELLED AS Eclipse watched with a grin. He waved his hand and Darcy turned off the device. Brant hung his head as he breathed harder and harder. This was the most pain he ever felt, like someone was squeezing all the light from him from the inside. Brant looked up at Eclipse who just glared back enjoying Brant's pain.

"You're strong," Eclipse said looking at Brant.

"Thanks," Brant replied with a smirk followed by more deep breaths.

"All this will end if you open the Stabilizer," he said trying to persuade Brant.

"Let me think about it. Um, no," he answered. Eclipse took a deep breath getting more and more frustrated with Brant.

"So be it," Eclipse said with another wave of his hand. Darcy flipped the same switch and the torture device started up again.

"Ah!" He yelled. "Ah!" Brant cried in pain, getting no sign of it stopping soon. Eclipse watched as Brant cried out in pain with a cold-blooded grin on his face while Darcy walked over to her father.

"He can't take much more of this," Darcy said standing next to her father. "He's going to keep refusing, and where does that get us?" She said frustratingly looking up at her father. Eclipse looked at Brant thinking of what to do, then his eyes lit up.

"You're right, Darcy," he said looking at her. "He may be unwilling, but he is still useful," Eclipse explained looking back at

Brant. "Turn it off," he ordered. Darcy walked back over to the panel and shut off the device. Brant hung his head with his eyes shut almost like he was unconscious, with blood dripping from his nose and the side of his mouth. Eclipse walked up to Brant and grabbed his chin, then moved it left and right looking him over. Eclipse raised his hand and a black dagger formed in his hand. Eclipse moved Brant's head to the left so he could see the right side of his head easier. He reached up and started to cut Brant's head making the hair on that side of his head fall off. The dagger cut the side of his head, even smoke could be seen as soon as it made contact with Brant. Even knocked-out Brant grit his teeth in pain as Eclipse moved the dagger in an arch-like motion, creating a deep cut on the side of Brant's head. Eclipse lowered his hand as he looked over the buzz cut he gave Brant. He bent down and picked up the hair he cut off, then he straightened up. "That wasn't so difficult, was it?" Eclipse asked with a grin, then he turned around and started to walk toward the cell door. "Get *The Embodiment* ready," he ordered.

"Yes, Father," Darcy replied as she followed. "But why did you do that?" She asked.

"Since the human was unwilling to work with us, I did the next best thing. We'll use his DNA to open the Stabilizer and it won't know the difference," Eclipse answered.

"That's why you cut his hair," Darcy said putting the pieces together.

"Yes, now that we have more than enough of his DNA we can move on," Eclipse replied. "Have everything prepared and ready to move," he ordered as they walked out into the gray hallway.

"Yes, Father," Darcy said with a bow. "What about him?" She asked looking back at Brant, then at her father.

"Leave him, just in case we need more of his DNA, and if we don't, we'll make him watch what we will do all because of him,"

Eclipse answered with a smile, then he turned and started to walk away as the door to Brant's cell closed behind them.

Two RAVEN GUARDS WALKED next to each other down the silver-plated hallway. They walked underneath an air vent, unknown to them they were being watched. The figure in the air ducts watched the troopers round the corner. Suddenly, the vent fell to the ground, but just before it hit the steel floor it lit up yellow, preventing the ear-pitching collision and alerting everyone that there was an uninvited guest. The vent gently landed and the light faded away with the passageway still empty. Alpha popped his head out of the air ducts with his head upside down. He looked behind him, then back in the same direction; he watched the guards walk to make sure the area was clear. He jumped out and landed with his legs separated so he wouldn't land on the vent he just dislodged.

"Okay, we're clear," he whispered up to the air vent.

"What would you have done if it wasn't?" Kit asked as she jumped down and stood next to her brother.

"Would it kill you to say *good job* every once in a while?" Alpha questioned back.

"Good job," Kit said with a smile rubbing Alpha's head.

"Okay, okay, don't patronize me," he replied taking a step to the side. Kit smiled as she watched Alpha gently swing his arm upward causing the air vent he just dislodged to light up yellow again and fly up and back into place erasing any suspicion of their presence. "Come on," Alpha said as he started to walk down the hall. Kit followed next to her brother as they looked around for guards.

"Anything?" She asked as they crept along.

"Nothing," Alpha answered. The two passed door after door but still nothing when, suddenly, the fur on the back of their necks stood up. They stopped and looked to their left, too, then at each other. "I'll get the door open," Alpha said walking over to a small panel while Kit watched their backs. "Make sure no one's coming," he said not realizing Kit was already doing it.

"Oh, that's a good idea," she said with a smirk. Alpha flipped a switch only a few seconds after he stepped in front of the panel making the cell door slide open. "Show off," Kit said with a grin as Alpha stepped by her side.

"What can I say, I'm the best," Alpha boasted. Kit rolled her eyes and smiled as the two started to walk into the small room, but when they saw Brant, they dropped their ears back.

"I'll get the restraints off," Kit said running over to the control panel while Alpha walked up to Brant. He looked up at Brant to see his mouth and nose bleeding along with hair shaved on one side.

"Oh, man, what did they do to you?" Alpha asked looking at him. Suddenly Kit deactivated the restraints letting go of Brant's wrists and ankles. Brant started to fall forward but Alpha caught him as he wrapped his arm around his shoulder. Kit ran up and looked at Brant with the same worried expression Alpha had as she looked him over.

"What did they do?" She asked looking at the scar on the side of his head.

"We got to get him out of here," Alpha said with his arm still wrapped around Brant.

"I'll make sure the coast is clear," Kit replied, then she turned and ran toward the door. She looked down both sides of the hallway as Alpha helped Brant to the door as his feet slid on the ground. They headed back down the hallway and underneath the vent they came out of only a minute or two ago. Kit reached her hand up and pulled downward causing the vent to fall again but this time she caught it.

"Here, I'll hold that; you go first," Alpha said reaching his hand out. Kit handed him the vent and jumped up into the ceiling.

"Okay, I'm ready," she said looking down at her brother. Alpha gently sat the vent down and used the same paw and held it out at Brant causing the air around him to light up. Alpha slowly and gently moved his paw upward toward the vent as Brant followed his motion. Kit grabbed Brant's arms as soon as they came within reach and pulled him inside. Just as soon as Brant was inside Alpha jumped inside the air ducts. He reached his paw down at the vent and pulled up like he was pulling a rope and the vent followed upward back into place.

"Come on, let's go," Alpha said as he started to crawl with his arm wrapped around Brant's shoulder guiding him through the vent system. They crawled through the maze of vents as they continued going out the same way they came in. They turned down another tunnel but this time a light could be seen at the very end. They crawled to the end of the metal tunnel and moved the vent out from its original place to reveal a way outside as the light poured in. Alpha leaned out and started to wave his hand back and forth as fast as he could. Then the sound of a ship grew louder and louder as it came into view. Alpha watched as it grew larger and larger till it stopped only a few feet from the palace. He watched as the ramp extended down making its way underneath the vent so they could get out while Solar was waiting for them inside.

"How'd it go?" Solar asked as Alpha crawled out and onto the ramp. Alpha looked at Solar with his ears back, then he bent down and helped Brant out. Solar's eyes got big when he saw the condition Brant was in. He ran down and took Brant's arm, and Alpha bent down and helped Kit out. Solar helped Brant inside the ship as Selene climbed down the ladder.

"Hey, how'd it—?" She started to ask but stopped when she saw Brant. She ran up to Brant as Solar gently lay him on the table. "What happened?" Selene asked Alpha and Kit as they walked in with the ramp closing behind them.

"I don't know," Alpha answered. Selene looked down at Brant with her ears back when, suddenly, an alarm blasted from the palace.

"I guess they noticed they're down a prisoner," Kit said trying to lighten the mood.

"Get us out of here," Selene said gesturing Alpha to head up to the cockpit.

"Got it," he replied as he ran past her. Selene watched Alpha climb up the ladder, then back down to Brant. Alpha climbed up and into the bridge where Crystal was in the pilot's seat. Crystal turned around and saw Alpha running up toward her.

"It's all you," she said getting out of the chair.

"Thanks," Alpha said as he sat down. He flipped a few switches, then he turned the ship around and sped off before Eclipse's men ever saw what happened.

J UST AS THE GROUP of outlaws flew away from Reavella the city stood in silence. An occasional horn blared for a second breaking the silence. The water just on the edge of the city stood so still you could see your reflection like a mirror. Suddenly the water started to become restless. The waves started to get larger and larger as a black object started to come into view from underneath the water. Just when everyone by the water stood and watched in wonder, a giant metal object crashed through the surface of the water. Everyone watched as a long black ship rose to the sky. The ship was black with a bright red light down the side. It was as long as it was wide casting a shadow underneath. The ship was full of soldiers and ready for battle. Near the center of the massive ship stood a tower that led up to the control room where four ravens sat by a circled control panel and the room ahead had a large glass window to see out into the world with a massive ship wheel and a raven-piloting station. Right in front of the window sat a circular stand that rose from the floor. The top of the stand was curved downward like a bowl with a bright blue circle surrounding its base. Eclipse started to walk up to the stand with the Reality Stabilizer in one hand and a handful of Brant's hair in the other as Darcy watched from his side.

"Father, I know your design and plan is greater than any of us could imagine," she started. "But what does it do?" Darcy asked. Eclipse smiled as he raised his hands, first the hand with the Stabilizer and placed it inside the bowl-like stand. The orb started to float as Eclipse divided up the hair in each hand and started to reach over at the golden object. He didn't even use his dark abilities just in case the Stabilizer would read it and know it wasn't Brant. Eclipse carefully grabbed both sides of the orb, twisted, and pulled. The Stabilizer opened and Eclipse's eyes lit up as it hovered in one spot with a light-blue light flowing from one end of the orb to the other. Eclipse smiled and looked out the window as he took a deep breath relieved it worked, but now it was time to get everything ready for the dark king to rise once again.

BRANT STARTED TO WAKE up with voices he could hear but his eyes were still closed. He moved his hands but, unlike earlier, he could move them without restraint; then, he moved his ankles to reach the same outcome. Brant shot up trying to escape the room, but he felt a stabbing pain in his head.

"Ow!" he said grabbing his head. Everyone ran over to Brant who was lying on the couch.

"It's okay, you're safe," Kit said kneeling by the couch. Brant opened his eyes again to see not only Kit but everyone as they stood in the house where he first met Selene.

"Kit?" Brant asked a little confused. He looked around as everyone gathered around the couch. "What happened? How'd I get here?" He asked.

"Don't worry about that," Kit answered with a soft grin. Brant sat up but grabbed his head still feeling the pressure from whatever Eclipse used on him.

"How do you feel?" Alpha asked.

"Okay, I guess," he answered. "If Eclipse does that to every prisoner, I'd hate to see his electric bill," Brant said trying to lighten the mood.

"You sure you're okay?" Selene questioned.

"I'm okay," Brant answered looking at her with a grin.

"Good," she replied with the same expression.

"Sorry," he apologized as he leaned forward grabbing his forehead for a moment. "I thought I could stop him."

"We all thought that at one point or another," Solar replied.

"Don't worry about it, you're safe now," Alpha reassured.

"Thank you," Brant thanked. He looked around the room but noticed one was missing. "Where's Crystal?" He asked.

"Back at the valley," Alpha answered. "She wanted to be with her people after Oath's passing," Alpha explained. Kit looked at the side of Brant's head to see his hair not only shaved but had a small curved scar that definitely wasn't there before.

"Brant, why did he shave the side of your head?" Kit asked making everyone look at his new, but not-so-good, haircut.

"He what?" Brant asked having no idea. He reached up and felt the side of his head to feel the shaved hair and the small scar from the dagger Eclipse used on him. "I thought I felt a draft," Brant joked making everyone laugh.

"Did he say why he would do that?" Selene asked.

"No," Brant answered. "By the time he did it I was out cold," he explained.

"Why would he do that?" Kit asked looking up at Selene who just shrugged her shoulders.

"The Stabilizer," Solar said getting everyone's attention. "Since Brant opened it the first time, only he could reopen it. Obviously. He refused so Eclipse used the DNA in his hair to unlock it. Now the orb will recognize it's still Brant wielding it instead of Eclipse," he explained.

"Oh, no," Brant said as he hung his head. "I blew it!"

"There's nothing you could've done," Selene said looking at Brant.

"No, but all of existence is going to suffer because of me," Brant replied.

"You did everything you could," Kit said seeing Brant getting frustrated with himself. "Trust me, we've all been there," Brant took a deep breath. He looked up at the group. If anyone could help him through this it would be them. He smiled as he stood up from the couch.

"Thanks," he said with a grin. "Why are we back here?" Brant asked.

"We needed a safe place to hide," Alpha answered.

"I bet everyone was happy to be back," Brant said with a grin, but he didn't get the response he thought. They all just looked at each other with a weary look across their faces. "What?" Brant asked.

"It's gone," Selene answered. "It's all gone," Brant looked at her with a look of disbelief. He slowly walked over to the door still weak from everything that happened as everyone watched but didn't stop him. Brant threw the door open but what he saw was worse than he thought. Brant's eyes got big as he stepped down and out of the house to see all the homes in The Hidden on fire. Brant looked to his left to see the same thing, homes blazing as everyone followed out. Brant walked to the edge of the concrete patio just outside the front door and stopped. He looked around to see the village destroyed as Selene walked up and stood next to him.

"He destroyed it all," Brant said in disbelief.

"All but our house," Selene added. "He wanted to make sure everyone knew whose fault this was," she said as Brant just looked out still in awe of what he saw. Brant just looked as the fires blazed.

"I was having fun at the beginning, finding a new place and figuring out its mystery," Brant started. "But now that Eclipse has what he wants no one is safe," he said taking a deep breath. "We have to stop him," he said. Selene looked over and smiled at him as Brant turned around facing the others.

"We won't be able to get inside the palace, not after we just snuck in and out," Alpha explained.

"He's not in the palace anymore," Brant started. "He's using a ship called *The Embodiment*, I heard him say that before you know I blacked out," he finished. They all looked at each other somewhat impressed.

"But Brant, there's only five of us, against an army," Kit replied.

"My mom once told me that life will throw everything it can at you, and the giants you'll face will always come larger than the one you already conquered; but, as long you have the right group of friends and just a little bit of light, you can do anything," he started. "We have more than we need to stop Eclipse," Brant finished. Selene looked at Brant and smiled.

"That was pretty good," Alpha said, breaking the silence.

"Right," Kit agreed.

"You heard him, get ready to go," Selene said with a grin. They all started to walk back inside as Selene stood next to Brant. "This is going to be fun," she joked. Brant looked at her and smiled, then over at Alpha who was about to step inside.

"Hey, Alpha," Brant said getting his attention. "You have a razor I can borrow?" He asked.

B RANT STOOD IN FRONT of the sink inside the twins' bathroom. It was a noticeably small room with just enough room for a small sink, shower, and commode. Brant reached down at the white porcelain top, grabbed the razor Alpha handed him a few moments ago, and closed the door to the room. He turned back around to face the mirror again and reached into his pocket. He pulled his phone out, placed it on the white surface that surrounded the sink, then unlocked his phone, opened his playlist, and selected a song by Stephen Stanley. Brant bent over the sink and started to cut his hair as a guitar melody started to play.

"*It's hard for me to believe that I have nothing to prove. I thought this dirt on my hands was going to keep me from you. I fall as much as I rise, feels like my walk is a crawl. When I'm alone in the night won't you leave the light on,*" the song played as Brant shaved the other side of his head, still bending over the sink as the chorus played with drums beating as hard as they could hit them. "*Cause I've been reckless with my heart, now I'm falling apart. I don't want to be the same, I need you to be the change. I surrender all I am. I know I've made mistakes, but the past will wash away. I'll do whatever it takes,*" the song played as Brant looked into the mirror. He turned his head to one side then the other to see the shaved sides. He reached his hands down and placed them underneath the faucet getting them soaked, and then he reached back up and pulled his hair back causing it to stick up. Brant looked over his hair and nodded thinking it wasn't terrible and started to walk out of the bathroom after placing his phone back in his pocket but kept the music playing as he slowly walked out of the room thinking about what they were about to do. *"Thought I was never enough. Heart has a way of its own, but I can lift up my eyes and know that you're in control. Sometimes I won't get it right. I'm gonna stumble and fall. When I'm alone in the night, I know you'll leave the light on,"* the song sang as it started to play the chorus again.

He walked down the hallway as the chorus played again with the guitar melody filling the dead noise. He opened the door getting everyone's attention. Selene looked at Brant just as he looked back at her. He shrugged his shoulders with a this-is-as-good-as-it's-going-to-get look. Selene smiled and nodded at Brant who nodded back, then she turned to everyone. She looked at everyone underneath the awning and nodded with a deep breath as the music played. Everyone started to walk to the road knowing what that gesture meant as the song reached the bridge with just instrumental music and a series of *ohs* that filled the village. They walked up to the ship that was sitting at the top of the hill with the ramp already down. Everyone walked up the ramp and over to the ladder that led up to the bridge. Just as they reached the top and found their seats, the song reached the end with just the singer singing with little to no instruments as the ship slowly moved upward.

"Cause I've been reckless with my heart, now I'm falling apart. I don't want to be the same, I need you to be the change. I surrender all I am. I know I've made mistakes, but the past will wash away. I'll do whatever it takes," just as the song finished the ship sped off toward Reavella.

40

"FIVE MINUTES," ALPHA SAID as he climbed down the ladder where everyone stood around the table at the center of the room as the ship flew itself. Kit reached down underneath the table and flipped a switch causing the lights to turn off and a bright blue hologram of Reavella appeared with all its skyscrapers and a giant ship floating above the skyline.

"Eclipse has all of his forces inside *The Embodiment*," Kit stated as everyone studied the hologram image.

"Which means the city is free from Eclipse's wrath," Solar added.

"That puts three times as many forces we have to maneuver around," Alpha said as the ship continued to fly.

"How do we get in?" Brant asked.

"There's a docking bay at the front of the ship," Selene started. "We can fly in and land without having any confrontation outside."

"The ship isn't sealed?" Brant questioned back.

"No one's crazy enough to try to infiltrate this thing," Alpha answered.

"But we are," Brant said with a grin. Kit smiled and shrugged her shoulders as Selene continued.

"The docking bay is equipped with scanners," she added. "So, anything that comes in they can read what's inside before the ship lands."

"We have smuggler hatches we can hide in. That shouldn't give us away," Solar explained.

"Getting in is the easy part," Kit replied. "Once we get in how will we know where the Stabilizer is stashed?"

"Last time, he kept it with him the whole time," Selene answered.

"But he has a second chance at the one thing he's never learned to let go of," Brant added.

"You're saying he might try something different?" Solar questioned.

"We shouldn't rule it out," Brant answered.

"So, how do we stop Eclipse if we don't know where the orb is?" Kit asked. At first, the room stood empty with just the sound of the ship's engine propelling the ship forward.

"We could disable the ship," Alpha said, breaking the silence. "If we make our way up to the bridge and shut everything down it would strand Eclipse and his army there."

"That could work," Selene whispered to herself. "There's a lift system just behind the tower holding up the bridge," she said pointing to it on the hologram. "If one of us can make it up there and shut everything down before Eclipse realizes we're there, we might have a chance."

"How are we going to get Eclipse's attention off us?" Brant asked.

"I can do that," Selene answered. They all looked at her wondering if she knew what she was signing up for.

"That wasn't what I was getting at," Brant replied.

"It's the only thing that would keep his attention," she explained.

"Yeah, but he blames you for losing the most important battle he's ever faced. Who knows what he'll do," he said hoping to change her mind.

"But it would work," Selene said making her mind up. "I'll surrender myself to Eclipse as Brant and Alpha make it to the bridge and, while they're doing that, Kit and Solar stay with the ship defending it just in case something goes sideways," she explained.

"What about you?" Kit asked.

"Stopping my father is what we should focus on," she answered.

"I'll come and find you after Alpha and I deactivate the bridge," Brant replied.

"Brant, that's not part of the plan," Selene said.

"It is now," he replied. Selene looked at Brant, at first slightly agitated at the fact he was going to compromise the outcome of the mission, but she remembered the conversation they had walking to the Valley of Light and knew his heart was in the right place.

"Okay," she said with a grin. Suddenly a beeping filled the room.

"We're here," Alpha said looking at Selene along with everyone else.

"Get ready," she said after taking a deep breath. Solar walked behind the ladder and opened a small, hidden door revealing a hidden compartment. He jumped in followed by Kit, then Alpha. Brant stepped up to the opening as Selene walked up to the ladder.

"Good luck," he said looking through the metal bars.

"If you can't find me in enough time, just leave," she reiterated.

"You don't have to worry about that, I'll find you," Brant reassured.

"Are all humans like you?" Selene asked with a grin.

"Nah, some aren't as optimistic, funny, outgoing, and humble as me," he answered with a smirk. "Come to think of it, I'm the total package, aren't I?" He said jumping down. Selene laughed as Solar reached up and closed the metal door while Selene climbed up the ladder. She made her way up to the bridge, walked up to the captain's chair, and sat down. She looked out the window to see *The Embodiment* flying over the city. Whether they came out on top or lost to the dark king it would all come down to today.

41

ELENE GLARED OUT THE window as she flew up to the massive ship. She took a deep breath as the ship flew slowly up to the massive docking bay entrance that acted as the only way in and out of *The Embodiment*. Selene looked up and to the right to see a scanner pointed down at her ship, then she looked to her right to see another scanner. Just next to the scanners were two balconies where ravens watched Selene as she slowly flew inside the ship.

"How many life signs are on that ship?" The raven asked from the balcony.

"One," the soldier answered. They all watched as Selene turned the ship around to face the massive circular opening before she landed the ship. The landing gear extended downward as the ship landed bouncing a few times as it settled on the ground as Selene sat in the captain's chair. She closed her eyes and took a deep breath again, then she unfastened her seatbelt and climbed down the ladder. The ramp extended downward as two ravens and Darcy walked up to the ship. They stopped as Selene walked down the ramp with her hands up. The raven guards looked at each other curiously as she walked up to them but Darcy's eyes never left her sister's.

"Take me to my father," she said holding her hands out together, ready for the handcuffs. Darcy looked at Selene with a smirk. She reached behind her with her hand open and the raven placed a pair of cuffs in the ghost's hand. Darcy strapped the cuffs on her sister's wrists and smiled as she made them as tight as she could. Selene started to walk with her hands now strapped with Darcy right behind her as they passed the guards.

"Great, now this going to mean nothing but paperwork," one of the guards complained as they started to follow Darcy and Selene. As they walked, Selene looked over her shoulder to see the ship appear to be empty.

"So far, so good," she thought to herself. The guards escorted Selene away as they rounded a corner. A few seconds passed as the ship stood still, till the floor started to move within the ship's walls. Suddenly, Solar climbed up, opening the hidden compartment with him. He looked around to see the coast was clear, at least for now.

"All clear," he said standing next to the hidden room. They climbed out of the smuggler hatch, first Alpha, then Kit, and finally Brant.

"I guess this is where we split up," Alpha said looking out of the ship, then back at everyone.

"Be safe," Kit said hugging her brother.

"Good luck," Brant said patting Solar on the back.

"You too," he replied with a smile as Alpha took a step away from Kit

"Ready?" Alpha asked Brant as they started to walk to the ramp. Brant nodded yes. The two started to walk down the ramp and into the massive station. Alpha peeked his head out first to make sure the coast was clear. "We're good, come on," he said taking a step or two away from the ship. Brant stepped out and his mouth dropped at the sight around him. The massive ship he was in had sleek black floors with orange lines outlining pathways. Brant looked up to see a conveyor belt attached to the ceiling with jets strapped to them as they moved to wherever they were supposed to go. Just underneath the conveyor belt were catwalks that looked like they weren't being used as they weaved around the ship ceiling. Alpha looked up to see the same walkway Brant saw. He followed a path back to them with a ladder just behind them attached to the wall. "Come on, this way," he said as he started to run toward the ladder. Brant looked around one last time still amazed at the sight, then he ran as he followed Alpha.

SELENE WALKED THROUGH THE massive flying station with Darcy with her hand at her back just to make sure she was walking in the right direction. Selene looked up to see fighter jets strapped to the ceiling and countless guards marching to the center of *The Embodiment*.

"Bring back some old memories?" Darcy asked her sister as they walked on the slick black-tiled floor.

"None of the good ones," she answered. Darcy smirked at her sister's back.

"Then why did you surrender?" Darcy questioned. Selene started to smile at the thought of Brant and Alpha running around the ship without Darcy or even her father having any clue about it, but she bit her lip and tried to come up with an answer that wouldn't give them away.

"I have my reasons," Selene answered. Darcy looked at Selene questionably but just let it go for the time being. They walked past a huge opening where countless ravens stood at attention. The two rounded a corner where a black stage sat with a black podium at its center. Eclipse was standing ready to address the crowd as Darcy led Selene behind the stage. He turned around to see his daughter handcuffed.

"After all these years," Eclipse said walking down the steps and down to their level. "The last time I saw you, I believe, you were stabbing me in the back. And if my memory is correct, it was on this very ship," Eclipse recalled looking down at Selene. "You went from daughter of the king to street mouse."

"I'll take that as a compliment," she defended. Eclipse took a deep breath and closed his eyes trying to keep his composure.

"I have something special planned this time," he said as he took the tips of his fingers and gently moved them in Selene's blond hair. "Take her upstairs and find the others," Eclipse said taking his hand away from Selene. "Now, you'll have to excuse me but you caught me just as I was about to address my biggest fans," he said with a cold grin. Eclipse turned around and walked up the small set of stairs as Darcy led Selene away. She looked at the ground thinking about that remark about finding the others.

"Did he know?" Selene asked herself as she walked. She looked back to see the stage Eclipse stood on rising like an elevator so the whole crowd could see him.

"Greetings, soldiers!" Eclipse shouted getting their attention, then he started to address the sea of ravens. "Together we have achieved a great many things. We have built an empire out of the ashes of this fallen world, but that was not our greatest achievement. With the success of the Purge, we eradicated the vermin that sought to hide their light from us, and now they are dust. Now I'm sure you have heard about the one Oath has proclaimed to stop us, but let me assure you this boy is not a threat to our great order," Eclipse said as Brant and Alpha moved on the catwalks far off in the distance at the far end of the crowd. "Brant Wilson!" He shouted. The two stopped and shot their heads over at the dark ruler not knowing what was happening. "Why haven't you stopped me yet?!" He shouted looking at the crowd. "Ha ha, yes," the crowd cheered as both Brant and Alpha took a sigh of relief but stayed on that spot overlooking the army as Eclipse continued.

"Years ago, we were on the eve of victory when we were be-trayed, and the last remaining Protectors thought they could keep us down. But now the key to our final victory is finally back in our possession," he said as he pointed up at the bridge and the ravens cheered again. Brant and Alpha turned around and looked up to see the Reality Stabilizer hovering over a silver bowl and, even worse, it was open. Suddenly, the ship shook for a moment. Alpha looked up to see the ship moving away from the city.

"We're moving," Alpha said as he looked up at the sky along with Brant then back down at Eclipse just as he started to ad-dress the army again.

"And, unlike the ancients who reserved this power for them-selves, I will open a hole in reality and from there our order will grow. There, the darkness will spread to every corner of reality," he said making the crowd cheer. "And we'll turn day to night for all time!" He shouted over the crowd.

"This is worse than last time," Alpha said with his ears back, then he took off running. Brant glared down at Eclipse, then followed behind Alpha as they heard Eclipse off in the distance.

"Prepare yourselves for a new era," Eclipse said as Brant ran away. "And with the death of my wife finally vindicated, I'll show the universe how strong I am and everything will be the way it was," he said looking over the crowd with a determined look while Brant caught up to Alpha on the catwalk.

"This is bad," Alpha said as they stopped at an intersection near the ceiling. Brant looked at Alpha with his eyes full of wor-ry over Eclipse's new plan. Brant looked down at the operation the dark king was running, then back up at Alpha.

"Get back to the ship and get ready for take-off," Brant start-ed but was cut off.

"That wasn't the plan," Alpha retaliated.

"Yeah, but that was before this curve ball," he replied.

"So?" Alpha questioned.

"We need to make sure everyone's ready to go," Brant answered.

"That's not part of the plan," Alpha explained.

"Would you knock it off, I'm not leaving till you guys are safe," Brant said getting to the point. Alpha looked at Brant and took a deep breath. He could see Brant meant what he said. "Get the ship ready when Selene and I—" Brant said as he started to run in the other direction, but Alpha grabbed his arm.

"Selene?" He asked letting go of Brant's arm. "What are you going to do?" Brant thought about a plan but couldn't come up with something.

"I'm a human, I'll improvise," Brant said with a smirk as he ran away from Alpha. Alpha watched as Brant dashed away, and then he turned and headed back in the same direction where he came from. Brant continued on the catwalks as the ship moved over the city as Eclipse's plan came closer and closer to fruition with every passing second.

4 3

B RANT RAN ACROSS THE catwalk as the troops below
started to stand at attention as the platform Eclipse stood
on lowered back down. Brant looked behind him just to
make sure he wasn't being followed or seen by any of Eclipse's
creeps in masks, then he took off again. He ran around a long
curved section of the high pathway as it worked its way behind
the tower that held up the bridge as Alpha made his way back
to the ship.

"What was he going do to?" Kit asked as they sat in their
ship's cockpit.

"He didn't feel the need to let me in on his plan," Alpha
answered.

"What about the rest of the plan?" She asked, realizing the
plan they came up with was already thrown out the window.
"How are we going to destroy this thing?" She asked. Alpha
looked at the floor while biting his lip trying to think of something. He looked out the window over to his right, and then
over at his left where the docking bay door stood still open.

"We've got missiles," he answered. "There's enough explo-
sives and combustible garbage around here we can use to our
advantage," Alpha explained. "Blow it up from the inside."

"And fly out before everything goes up in flames," Kit finished with a smirk liking that plan more than the original. "But
first we have to wait for Brant and Selene."

"Obviously," Alpha replied. "That's not exactly helpful," he said with a smirk stating the obvious. Kit smiled and rolled her eyes.

"Why not blow up the ship now?" Solar asked missing the conversation even though he was only a row behind.

"We just established that blowing up the ship while the team is still inside isn't exactly helpful," Alpha answered.

"When did we establish that?" Solar questioned back.

"Like three seconds ago," Alpha answered amazed he was having this conversation again.

"I wasn't listening, I was thinking of something else," he said leaning back in his seat. Kit rolled her eyes as Alpha shook his head for a moment, then looked out of the window.

"Don't worry, they'll make it," Alpha reassured looking up at the catwalk where he left Brant.

Brant ran as fast as he could around the long, rounded corner that led to the back of the tower. He slowed down as he finally arrived there. Brant stopped at a ledge when the pathway he was on stopped suddenly. He looked up to see a lift coming down on a ribbon of blue light, then he looked down to see a separate platform making its way up like a pulley system. Brant hopped across the small gap as the platform made its way upward. He looked down at the catwalk he just stood on as he continued to move upward. Brant looked up just as the platform started to slow down alongside a standing platform with a light gray door. He jumped off the lift and onto the more stable platform. Brant looked behind him to see Reavella shining in the distance as the ship continued to move. He took a step forward and the doors slid open to reveal a small hallway. He walked down the hallway and up to another set of doors. The doors slid open and Brant stepped inside the room to see four circular desks and ravens sitting. The raven closest to the door looked behind him to see a human standing in the doorway. He flipped a switch making a beeping sound, then a cage shot from the floor surrounding the desk. Suddenly three more cages arose protecting the other ravens, then they started working again as if Brant wasn't there. Brant looked ahead to see two small closet-size doors open and two ravens stepped through.

"Identify yourself, citizen," the raven ordered. Brant looked at the ravens and his hands lit up yellow. The soldiers saw the light and drew their blasters as fast as they could grab them.

"I'm not a citizen, I'm a Protector," Brant said with a grin, then he threw his arm out at the ravens as they opened fire. The raven pilot turned around from the next room with his hands still on the wheel. He heard the sound of combat but he couldn't leave his post. He watched as the door opened and a raven screamed and hit the ground, then Brant walked in. Brant looked over at the pilot but didn't touch him since he was already occupied. Brant walked up to the silver bowl in front of the window overlooking *The Embodiment*. He looked down at the Reality Stabilizer in it wide open. He looked over at the raven to see if he was going to pounce on him but he didn't move, it just watched Brant. Brant looked back at the Stabilizer and gently reached his hands down at it. He grabbed both sides of the orb and slid it shut, twisted the sides locking it back shut, and removed it from the bowl. As soon as he removed the Stabilizer from its slot an alarm erupted throughout the ship. Eclipse looked up at the bridge and grunted in frustration as he started to walk faster. Just as Brant was about to turn around, he heard the faint beep of an elevator. He turned around just as the doors to the hallway slid open to see Darcy and Selene handcuffed.

"Brant," Selene said, seeing him still in the room with the Stabilizer in his hand. "Run!" She shouted. Darcy pushed

Selene down, then she jumped up and whipped her feet making her float like a ghost. Brant's grip grew tighter on the orb. Suddenly, he started to run toward Darcy, then she flew toward Brant with a cold grin on her face ready for the fight, but right before Brant made his way to the ghost, he tossed the Stabilizer up in the air. Darcy's eyes got big as she gasped watching the orb fly in the air. With the attention off him, Brant reached his hand out and Darcy shot backward. She flew back making the doors to the outside lift slide open, and she flew just past the edge. She looked up just as Brant reached his hand up again but, this time, he pulled his hand down like he was pulling hard on a rope. Suddenly, Darcy flew down hitting her head on the ledge. Brant watched as she fell from the impact. He ran over to Selene and helped her up from the floor. He reached two of his fingers up, flicked his wrist making a bright yellow beam appear, and sliced through the silver binders freeing her.

"Time to get out of here," Brant said running over and grabbing the Stabilizer off the floor.

"But Eclipse is on his way, we don't have time," Selene replied.

"Come on," Brant said with a smile. He took off running back toward the massive window with Selene right behind him. Brant grabbed the raven who was piloting the ship and threw his hand out at the window making a bright yellow beam shoot out shattering the window. Just before he got to the window, Brant reached back and grabbed Selene's hand and pulled her close as they jumped. Selene held on to Brant with a death grip as they fell. Just before they hit the ground, Brant forced the wings of the raven guards out and they started to glide down. They hit the ground and rolled a few feet.

"Come on!" Solar shouted from the ramp of their ship. "Hurry!" He shouted as they started to get up.

"Told you so," Brant said with a smirk, and in the same tone Selene said it to him back at The Hidden. She watched Brant run toward the ship with a smile, then she took off behind him. They ran up the ship's ramp and up the ladder that led to the much smaller bridge as the ramp closed sealing the ship. Brant climbed up with Selene and Solar right behind him. Kit and Alpha turned around as they all got in their seats. "You might want to hold on to this," he said with a grin tossing the golden orb at Kit. Kit caught the Stabilizer and looked over at her brother impressed.

"Show off," Alpha replied.

"That wasn't bad," Brant said impressed with himself.

"I could've done better," he said with a smirk.

"Alpha," Kit interjected. "Can we get out of here, or are we going to wait until they start shooting at us?"

"Where's your sense of fun?" Alpha questioned back as he started to power the ship up.

"Outside of the ship," Kit answered.

"Agreed," everyone said at the same time.

"Yeah, yeah, I'm on it," Alpha replied as the ship started to move upward.

44

D ARCY SHOT BACK UP after getting hit hard. She flew up to the bridge to see it empty as she moved down the hallway. She looked around while she whipped her tail and her feet reappeared again. Darcy ran up to the massive window that was now shattered at its center. She looked at the window, and then over at the bowl where the Stabilizer once stood.

"Darcy," she heard. Darcy turned around to see her father walking to her with a group of guards. He walked into the room looking over the shattered window. "Where are they?" He questioned.

"I don't know," Darcy answered reluctantly. Eclipse looked at the ground making a grunting noise as he bit his lip when, suddenly, they heard the sound of a ship powering up. Eclipse took a step to the broken glass to see a bright white-and-blue ship start to take off. "Stop them!" He shouted.

"Go, go, go!" Darcy yelled at the raven guards just standing around. The guards jumped through the shattered glass diving down to the ship as Alpha lined up the ship from the driver's seat ready to get to his favorite part of the plan.

"You want to do the honor?" Kit asked looking over at her brother.

"It would be my pleasure," Alpha answered flipping a switch next to the joystick and a click sounded on the wings of the ship. "Oh, yeah," Alpha said with a smirk, as he pressed the small red trigger on the joystick. Two purple missiles shot from the wings of the craft making their way to the center of the ship. The missiles struck a column near the stage Eclipse just made his big speech making an explosion rupture. "Woohoo!" Alpha cheered as he continued to shoot. He slowly turned the ship till he made his way to the support beam that held up the bridge. He smirked out the window seeing an opportunity he couldn't pass up. Alpha pulled the trigger and two more missiles shot out hitting the base of the bridge as it started to rupture.

"Nice shot," Brant said with a grin as the ship turned toward the docking bay door. "Did you know that was a weak spot or did you guess?" He asked.

"Of course. Why do you think I did it in the first place," Alpha said with a smirk. "Now, if you don't mind, I'm going to direct us out before everything goes up in flames," he said sarcastically.

"You guessed, didn't you?" Selene questioned back.

"He did," Kit answered with a smile looking over to see Alpha trying to come up with a comeback.

"You could've told me I did a good job," he replied with a smirk.

"Get us out of here first," Kit said as flames started to burst around them. Alpha pulled a lever forward and the ship took off out of *The Embodiment* while Eclipse watched the ravens he sent down fly backward with the suction of the ship taking them with them. Before he could shout more orders, the base of the bridge exploded causing everything to shake. Eclipse started to fall but regained his balance, and then he looked out the opened window with a look of worry on his face. Darcy looked over at her father as the ship started to move downward after losing connection from the bridge.

"Detach," Eclipse said looking over at Darcy. She ran up a slope as the flying fortress started to fall on its side. Darcy grabbed the wheel of the ship and moved her hand down by the base of the post holding up the steering mechanism where a red button sat with a plastic cover over it. She flipped open the plastic cover and pushed the small red button. Suddenly, the bridge started to power up as smoke was released from underneath the main part of the platform as it started to hover over the burning wreckage.

"We're clear," Darcy said as she steadied the ship. Eclipse looked down at the burning wreckage as it started to land in the water. He looked behind him and out a small window on the door to where the lift system once led to see the ship Selene escaped in getting away.

"After them," Eclipse said in a soft tone trying to keep his composure. Darcy turned the wheel till it lined up with the escaping ship and started to pursue them as what was left of *The Embodiment* burned behind them.

45

BRANT LOOKED OUT THE window just as Eclipse followed behind with *The Embodiment* burning into a blaze. He looked over at Selene who was just looking down at the floor with her eyes moving from side to side.

"What's wrong?" Brant asked seeing something was on her mind.

"That was too easy," she answered looking up at him.

"You think that was easy?" Brant questioned back with a grin. Suddenly the fur stood up on the back of Selene's neck just as Brant felt the hair on the back of his head shoot up. Selene grabbed the small digital pad by her chair and opened it to a camera view from the back of the ship.

"Oh, no!" she said dropping her ears back as Eclipse pursued.

"Fire," Eclipse ordered. Darcy pressed a small button next to her pink thumb and fired two heat-seeking missiles.

"Alpha, move!" Selene yelled but it was too late. The missiles struck the right wing of the ship as it exploded making the ship fall from the sky.

"Oh, okay," Brant said to himself as he held onto the arms of his seat. He watched out the window as the ship sped toward the ground.

"Time to handle a crash landing, just like I taught you," Alpha said from the front seat.

"When did you teach me?" Brant questioned back.

"I didn't, just a little team building before we have a bad landing," he answered.

"You mean crash landing!" Kit corrected.

"I was trying to put a positive spin on it," Alpha replied. The ship crashed on a beach just off the city's edge. The ship slid on the dark blue sand, and then it stopped as smoke filled the area while Eclipse looked down from his ship.

"Land the ship," Eclipse ordered looking down at the ship through the shattered glass.

NSIDE THE SHIP, BLACK smoke filled the bridge of the once-flying ship. Brant started to wake up opening his eyes just a little to see nothing but smoke. He looked over at Selene's chair to see her slouched over. He unfastened his seatbelt and walked across the floor which now sat at a forty-five-degree angle. Brant leaned against her chair as Kit got up from her seat and turned around to see everyone but Brant not moving.

"Come on, come on, let's move," Kit said walking up to her brother. "Alpha, come on!" she said grabbing him by the shoulders and shaking him.

"Hmm, what? What happened?" Alpha asked waking up.

"The ships smoking, what do you think happened?" Kit questioned back. "Get Solar," she said unfastening his seat belt.

"Got it," he replied as he slowly got to his feet. Brant moved Selene's safety restraints out of the way and gently moved her toward him. He slowly and gently picked her up and wrapped one of her arms around his neck. He looked up to see Kit and Alpha helping Solar up.

"How do we get out of here?" Brant asked.

"We'll go through the front," Alpha answered. Brant looked ahead to see the window positioned down at the ground facing the blue sand except for the very top of the window with its glass shattered as they heard the sound of the city off in the distance. "You, okay?" He asked Solar as he got to his feet.

"Yes," he answered rubbing his shoulder.

"Let's move," Kit said trying to keep everyone moving. She walked up to the window with everyone right behind her. They all walked with a limp or pain of some kind as they crawled through the broken glass. Brant helped Selene through the glass handing her to Alpha who was waiting. After handing her to Alpha, Brant crawled through the window as more glass fell from the ship. Kit and Solar climbed down with Brant behind them. Brant reached the beach floor and turned around as Alpha started to hand Selene down to him. He reached up and grabbed Selene and put her arm around his neck. Alpha climbed down and the three started to hobble away from the wreckage when Selene started to wake up. She looked down at the sand as her feet dragged along, and then up at Brant.

"What happened?" She asked waking up.

"Well, the plan took a turn we weren't planning on," Brant answered.

"How?" She questioned back. "What went wrong?"

"It crashed and burned at the end," he answered with a smirk. Selene looked up at Brant, smiled, and rolled her eyes while laughing quietly. They walked along the blue sanded beach when a ship started moving down to the beach. Everyone looked up as the ship started to land. They watched as the ship flew down, the landing gear stretched down, and the ship settled on the beach. Brant watched a ramp extend down to the ground and, not long after, Eclipse walked out with Darcy. "What do we do?" Brant asked.

"He can't get the Stabilizer," Selene answered. "Who has it?"

"I do," Kit answered.

"Give it to me," Brant said looking back at Kit. Selene looked at Brant thinking he had lost his mind. "You, guys, are beat up. If this does come down to a fight, I'm best equipped to fight

Eclipse right now," he explained reaching his hand out. Kit looked at Selene who nodded in agreement, and she handed the orb to Brant. Brant took the orb and looked back at Eclipse who was walking up to the group of outcasts.

"That was quite a display of heroism," Eclipse said standing only a few feet away from everyone. "Now, hand over the Stabilizer, Wilson," he said holding out his hand.

"How dumb do you think I am?" Brant questioned. "You think just by walking up and asking I would just do it because you asked?" He said shrugging his shoulders in disbelief.

"I wasn't asking," Eclipse said making a fist. Suddenly, black sand wrapped around Selene squeezing her.

"Hey!" Kit yelled but Eclipse was ready. He waved his other hand and sent everyone flying separating them. Brant flew by the water rolling to a stop just before the waves crashed on the shoreline. He looked up to see Eclipse looking down at him with his hand still out at Selene as she screamed in pain. Brant looked over at Selene, and then back at Eclipse.

"Open the Stabilizer and hand it over, then I'll let her go," Eclipse said looking at Brant. Brant got to his feet and looked over at Selene with the Stabilizer still in his hand. He looked at the dark king, grabbed the orb with two hands, and opened it like he did back on Earth. The Stabilizer opened and a bright blue sphere shone at its center. Eclipse extended his other hand and made the orb float on a cloud of black sand making its way to him. The golden orb made its way to Eclipse's hands as he let go of Selene. She fell to the ground as Eclipse held the Stabilizer with both hands. Brant ran over to Selene and got down on his knees as she coughed up sand.

"Are you okay?" He asked as the others made their way back to them. She looked up at Brant and nodded yes, and then she looked up at her father.

"Oh, no!" She said realizing what was in his hands. Eclipse closed his eyes and, at first, nothing happened. Suddenly a door shattered behind him as it opened for all to see. It looked like a gateway that shattered open like glass behind him and inside the shattered archway was a pink-and-blue cast with small formations like clouds but it was hard to make out. Eclipse opened his eyes to see everyone staring back at him.

"Take a good look around you, Selene, because your reality is about to change," Eclipse said with a grin as he took a step back into the portal with Darcy right behind him, then everything stood silent.

"Wait here," Brant said as he started to walk to the shattered opening.

"You're not going in there alone," Selene said grabbing his arm.

"This is my fault. I was the one who brought the Reality Stabilizer in the first place," he replied.

"You may have started it, but we'll finish it together," Selene said standing up. "Your mom said all we need is each other, right?" She said remembering what Brant said back at The Hidden. Brant took a deep breath looking at everyone standing in front of him.

"Right," he answered with a grin.

"You want to lead us in?" Selene asked with a soft grin. Brant turned around and looked at the portal, and then turned back around one more time.

"Try to keep up," he said with a smile as he took off running. Selene smiled as she looked back at the others and started to move.

"Here we go," Kit said shrugging her shoulders in disbelief and took off running with her brother and Solar right behind her. Brant crossed the blue-sanded beach and jumped through the shattered gateway with everyone else right behind him.

RANT JUMPED THROUGH THE shattered doorway with everyone right by his side. He looked down as he started to fall into the unknown till his feet landed on glass. Brant looked up at his new surroundings to see the sky in this shattered reality a bright blue and pink mixed. He looked back down at his feet to see glass making it appear he was standing in the air as the warped-looking sky surrounded him in this shattered reality.

"Okay, this is cool," Brant said looking back up.

"Selene," Solar said looking straight ahead. They all looked ahead to see Eclipse with his back turned to them and Darcy right by his side. Selene started walking slowly toward her father. Darcy turned around at the sound of footsteps glaring at the group. Eclipse looked at Darcy but didn't turn around.

"You sure are tenacious, I'll say that," Eclipse said knowing they were close. "But now it's time to begin again," Eclipse said opening the orb. Suddenly the sky shattered like glass as portals opened to countless worlds. They all looked up in awe, amazed by what they were seeing.

"Let's get him," Alpha said as they started to run but Selene held her arms out stopping them from continuing forward.

"This is mine," she said never taking her eyes off Eclipse. When Eclipse heard this, he turned around facing her and the others not too far behind. "Not bad for an old man," Selene said with a smile walking closer.

"Do I look the part?" Eclipse asked with a smile but it was a sincere smile.

"No, you don't look so bad," Selene answered with a smile.

"After all these years, where did we end?" Right back where we started," Eclipse said walking toward Selene.

"Looks like it," she replied.

"You promised me when we started this seven years ago, we would do this together. You broke your promise and ran," Eclipse said stopping a few feet from Selene.

"I know I did," she replied. "But once I saw what you wanted to do to with the Stabilizer I couldn't just sit back and watch," Selene explained as everyone watched with tension running high.

"You would've been safe," he snapped.

"But for how long?" Selene questioned back. "I saw what you did to the Protectors, and I know what I did for you in the Purge!"

"The Purge only happened because they refused to help your mother!" Eclipse yelled.

"Did you ever stop to think they couldn't help her?" Selene asked. "The light's abilities are vast but the power of healing doesn't come from it. Believe me, if there was a chance to save her, don't you think I would've?"

"How would I know?" Eclipse questioned back rather quickly. "You betrayed me and ran away with a group of outlaws."

"It was the only choice I had," she defended.

"You had a choice!" He replied. "Now you will be dealt with just like your friends, as a traitor." Eclipse said looking into Selene's eyes. She looked down at the ground for a moment trying to wrap her head around what her father was implying.

"Okay, can you just put all that aside for a second and be my dad?" Selene asked taking a deep breath. "I lost Mom, but

I never meant to lose you, too," she said looking at her father. Eclipse looked down at the ground and took a deep breath.

"You will be dealt with like the others," Eclipse said still looking at the ground.

"What?" Selene asked in disbelief. "Dad, are you that afraid of me?" She asked as Brant watched Eclipse close his fist.

"Oh, no," he said remembering his brief fight with the dark king back at the valley.

"Dad?" Selene asked trying to get through to him but it was too late. Suddenly Eclipse threw his fist down and a wave of black sand appeared hurling over Selene and making its way to Brant and the others.

"Look out!" Brant yelled jumping back. The wave just missed Brant's foot shattering the glass beneath their feet.

"No!" Selene yelled as they fell.

"Finish them off," Eclipse ordered Darcy.

"Yes, Father," Darcy said after hesitating. She whipped her feet making her ghost body float again as she pursued after the others while Selene watched as everyone fell underneath a blue-and-pink cloud.

B RANT FELL UNDERNEATH THE blue-and-pink clouds with Kit, Solar, and Alpha by his side. Kit looked up to see the shattered glass that made up the platform they were formerly standing on. She reached her hand up making the shattered glass light up as they all continued to fall, then she threw her arm downward with her hand open. Brant watched the broken glass hurl past him and form another platform a few feet away. He straightened his legs as they made their way to the patched-up landing platform. He landed on the glass plat-form as Solar landed on the farthest side while Alpha and Kit landed only a few feet away. Brant looked down at his feet to see the broken platform with all its pieces put together like a puzzle of a stained-glass window.

"Show off," Alpha said with a grin as they all walked up to each other.

"You could've said *thank you*," Kit replied with the same smile.

"It's very rude," Solar chimed. Alpha looked at him out of the corner of his eye with a smirk.

"Yeah, you should've started with *thank you*, and then go in with *show-off*," Brant added. Alpha shook his head with a smirk on his face.

"Thank you," he said after rolling his eyes.

"There you go," Kit said with a smile enjoying harassing her brother.

"Too bad it wasn't heartfelt," Brant joked.

"Can we focus on getting back up to Selene," Alpha replied changing the subject.

"We better hurry," Kit added when they heard a voice from behind.

"I wouldn't get your hopes up if I were you," Darcy said making everyone turn around.

"Oh, great! The Halloween decoration's back," Brant said as they all watched Darcy float down.

"Hello, Brant," Darcy said only a few feet from them. "My father has sent me to make sure you don't interfere with his plans."

"He should've thought of that before he strapped me to a chair and shaved the sides of my head," he replied.

"I like what you did with it," Kit added. Brant looked over and nodded with a smile, then he looked back at Darcy.

"So, what are you going to do?" Brant asked.

"Well, like father, like daughter," Darcy said with a smile, then she flew underneath the glass platform.

"Oh, this can't be good," Alpha said, looking underneath the glass but everything was distorted. Suddenly, Darcy crashed through making a hole in the glass. She swung her tail where her feet should've been hitting Solar and Alpha. "Whoa!" Alpha yelled sliding across the glass faster than he expected with Solar behind him. He started to slide off the edge when he grabbed the ledge of the glass. Solar started to fall off the edge right next to him, but Alpha grabbed him by the hand while holding on to the platform with only one hand.

"Alpha," Kit whispered to herself seeing he was in trouble. She started to run to him but Darcy wrapped her ghostly tail around her neck.

"That's not going to happen," Darcy whispered into Kit's ear with an evil grin, but Brant jumped and swung his foot hitting the ghost in the back of the head making her let go of Kit. Darcy hit the glass platform and rolled a few inches as Brant helped Kit to her feet.

"You, okay?" He asked.

"Yeah," Kit answered looking back to see Alpha still hanging on but not by much.

"I'll get Alpha and Solar while you take care of our flying friend," Brant explained, and then he started to run toward Alpha. Kit watched Brant take off as Darcy got back up. She turned around in time to see Darcy flying toward her. She ducked just as the young ghost hurled over her swinging her hand but missed. Kit straightened up just as Darcy was turning around and threw her light at her hitting her in the side. She hit the ground but she got back up and flew at Kit again as Brant ran over to Alpha and Solar.

"Hang on," Alpha said to Solar trying to figure out what to do since he was below the platform he couldn't see Brant coming. He looked at the piece of glass he was holding on to see it start to break off from the pressure of the two holding on. "Oh, come on," he said to himself.

"What are you doing up there?" Solar asked holding on to Alpha's hand with an unknown abyss beneath him.

"Nothing, that's the problem," he answered. Suddenly, the glass gave way and they started to fall. "Ah!" Alpha started to yell but they stopped falling as the air around them lit up yellow from the light. They looked up to see Brant holding his hands out with his eyes closed. Brant slowly started to move his arms backward making Alpha and Solar move upward toward the platform.

"I knew he could do it," Solar said looking up.

"We all knew," Alpha said with a soft grin as he reached his hand up at Brant. Brant opened his eyes and started to reach his hand down to Alpha as Kit held off Darcy. Darcy fell to the ground again with her head facing Brant. She looked up to see Brant helping Alpha and Solar up.

"He's figuring it out!" She yelled in frustration as she started to fly toward them. Kit looked past Darcy to see Alpha getting back up on the shattered glass but Darcy was coming and all their backs were turned leaving them open.

"No!" Kit yelled as she reached her hand down by her side. The glass by her foot lit up yellow just as Kit threw shards of glass at her. Darcy looked behind her just as glass flew by her head. Some pieces missed but others didn't.

"Ah!" She yelled in pain as glass hit her arms and legs. Everyone turned around as Kit reached down for another piece of glass and threw it up at Darcy but, instead of hitting her, it hit her dress pinning her to the platform. She tried to move as Kit ran past her.

"Are you okay?" Kit asked hugging her brother.

"I'm okay," he answered. Kit turned around to see Brant watching.

"Thank you," Kit said with one arm still around Alpha. Brant smiled and nodded his head.

"You did good," Solar said patting Brant on the shoulder a little harder than Brant was expecting.

"Thanks," Brant said with a smile when, suddenly, they heard Darcy laugh from behind.

"You, honestly think this is over?" She asked.

"No, this is just round one," Brant answered.

"You can't beat him," she said looking up at Brant.

"Not alone," Brant started as he got on one knee so he would be close to Darcy. "You may not have had a choice the first time, but now you do," he said reaching his hand out and removing the shattered glass that was pinning her dress to the ground with his light. Darcy looked down at her dress that was now free, and then up at Brant amazed at what he did. "Help us," Brant said with a gentle smile.

"I—" Darcy started trying to find the words. "I can't," she said flying upward but stopped to look back. "I'm sorry," she said taking a deep breath.

"Hopefully we'll see you around when this is all over," Brant said with a smile. Darcy smiled back and nodded, and then she flew up passing the clouds making her way back to the doorway that led to Reavella.

"Why did you just let her go?" Alpha asked as they walked up to him.

"My mom taught me everyone deserves a second chance," he started. "Selene gave Eclipse his chance and he turned it away, but no one gave her one," Brant explained. Alpha looked over at Kit and smiled and Solar nodded his head in agreement. "Speaking of Eclipse, we need to get back up there and help Selene," Brant said looking up.

"This is the easy part," Kit said with a grin. She waved her hands first starting from the ground, and then moved them upward making the glass move as she shaped a series of blocks floating in the air making their way back up to Eclipse and Selene. "After you," Kit said with a grin. Brant smiled back as he jumped up to the first block with Kit, Alpha, and Solar right behind him making their way back up to Eclipse and Selene.

SELENE WATCHED EVERYONE FALL underneath the clouds as Darcy pursued them vanishing out of sight.

"Looks like it's just you and me," Eclipse said with Selene still looking down. She turned around just in time to see Eclipse reach down to grab the blue orb at the Reality orb's center. Selene stood up as fast as she could and swung her arm at Eclipse making a bright beam of light appear as it flew toward the dark king. The beam struck the orb knocking it out of Eclipse's hands. Just as the Stabilizer hit the ground Selene ran at her father, jumped up, and swung her leg hitting him in the head creating a gap between him and the orb. Selene watched as he stood back up as Eclipse's eyes locked with hers. "You should've walked away while you were still ahead," he said clenching his fist.

"Well, you can't please everyone," Selene replied with a smirk.

"Ah!" Eclipse yelled in frustration throwing a black arrow at Selene. She ducked under as it flew over her head, but Eclipse wasn't done yet. He waved his hand up causing black sand to shoot through the cracks of the glass of the platform. Selene jumped back and moved her hand diagonally across her body slicing the pillar in half. The black sand fell back through the cracks in the glass but, as the sand subsided, Eclipse jumped through the falling sand swinging his arm and catching Selene off guard. He struck Selene on the cheek sending her flying back to the edge of the platform. Selene landed on one knee as she slid to a stop. She stood back up while Eclipse walked through the last of the black sand. Before any of the two could retaliate, Darcy flew up and headed toward the gateway that led back to Reavella. "Darcy?" Eclipse asked getting her attention. Selene turned around and looked up at Darcy as she hovered by the gateway. Darcy looked down at Selene and smiled a sincere smile. Selene looked up at Darcy and smiled back and nodded her head. Darcy nodded back and flew through the portal leading back home. Selene just stared at the portal trying to think of what would cause that outcome, but it didn't take her too long to figure out.

"Thanks for giving her a second chance Brant," Selene said with a smile knowing he had something to do with it. Suddenly, black sand wrapped itself around Selene's arms constricting her from moving. "Hey!" She shouted trying to break free. She turned her head just enough to see Eclipse holding his hand out toward her with his fist closed. Before she had a chance to get free, Eclipse swung his hand up in the air making the pillar of black sand follow. Then Eclipse swung his arm down as hard as he could away from the portal causing his power to follow suit. Selene flew down and hit the glass platform cracking it, but didn't fall completely through. Selene started to open her eyes as the sand that was wrapped around her body moved to her hands and feet. She opened her eyes to see Eclipse standing over her, and then he started to move his hand upward making a new pillar appear, but this one was different. She watched as a dagger formed at its tip and slowly moved downward till it pointed down at Selene. She tried to break free but couldn't as Eclipse glared down at her with the Reality Stabilizer in his hand.

"I'm sorry, Selene," Eclipse said, but before he could make his move a bright beam shot out from behind, hitting Eclipse in the back sending him flying away from Selene, dropping the orb. The dagger made of black sand lost its form and fell to the ground covering the area in a black haze. Selene looked up to see who saved her but couldn't see at first, but as the black mist started to clear she could make out a human's outline.

S ELENE WATCHED THE ORB roll beside her as it came to a slow stop. She reached over and grabbed the golden sphere and stood back up while everyone made their way to her.

"No need to thank me," Brant said with a grin as they stood around. "So, now what?" He asked.

"This is it," Selene answered with a look of sadness in her eyes. Brant looked at her at first confused. "You can go home," she finished looking at the portals. Brant looked around trying to find the gateway that led back to San Fransisco but it was hard to see with the sky full of portals. He turned around still looking up but when he looked straight ahead, he saw the orphanage which he called home through a portal standing next to the portal that led back to Reavella. At first Brant smiled seeing his home again but once he realized this was it the smile on his face melted away.

"Oh," Brant said as he turned back around to face everyone. "I guess this is it," he said looking up at the group. Brant watched Alpha as he walked up to Brant.

"See you around," Alpha said reaching his hand out. Brant smiled and grabbed the fox's hand, but Alpha pulled bringing Brant in for a hug that he wasn't expecting. "Stay out of trouble," he said letting go and taking a step back. Brant nodded with a soft smile as Kit walked up.

"Thanks for your help in getting away from the ravens when we first met," Brant said hugging Kit.

"We're just lucky we got to you first," Kit replied taking a step back. "But next time think about what you're doing instead of running all crazy," she said trying to lighten the mood.

"Fair," Brant said with a laugh as Solar walked up. "See you later, big guy," he said as Solar hugged him. At first, Solar didn't say anything as he took a step back.

"It was fun," he said with a small smile.

"It was, wasn't it," Brant replied with a smile seeing Solar was being sincere. Brant looked over as Selene walked up with the Reality Stabilizer still in her hands. Brant just looked at her with a gentle grin as she handed him the orb.

"You know, you don't have to leave," Selene said as everyone stood behind her. "You're welcome to stay with us," she said with a grin. Brant looked at her surprised by the thought of her wanting him to stay. He looked at the group who shared the same opinion. "Your world may not want you, but we do," she said. Brant tried to find the words, but he was so taken aback by the moment he couldn't find them. Brant turned around to look at the portal that led back to the orphanage and Mr. Sim standing outside hearing the whole thing. He smiled and nodded his head as the others tried to convince Brant.

"The only repercussion would be Solar having a roommate," Kit added with a smile as Brant turned back around to face them.

"It would be an honor," Solar said with a smile.

"Stay," Selene said convincing Brant. Brant smiled but right before he gave his answer, they heard a shout behind him.

"Enough!" Eclipse yelled, making everyone turn around. "You're not going anywhere!" He shouted as he stood on a pillar of black sand.

"Get out of here, I'll take care of him," Brant said taking a step or two toward Eclipse.

"Wait, what are you going to do?" Selene asked grabbing him by the arm. "Do you even have a plan?"

"Half of one," Brant answered with a grin.

"Half?" Selene questioned back.

"Hey, I learned from the best," he said with a smile. Selene looked at Brant trying to come up with what he was thinking but couldn't.

"We can do this together," she insisted.

"I know but Eclipse and I are the only ones who can control the Reality Stabilizer in here. So, the best way for me to help you is by keeping you safe," Brant explained. Selene looked at Brant while taking a deep breath. "Trust me."

"Okay," she agreed with a gentle smile. "Let's get out of here before Brant blows everything up," Selene said as she started to run toward the portal. Brant followed everyone back till he reached the edge of the glass platform. He watched as Kit jumped through followed by Alpha, and then Solar; but Selene stopped right before she reached the edge of the platform. "You never told us if you were staying."

"I guess you'll have to find out," Brant answered with a smirk.

"See you around," Selene said with a smile. Brant smiled as he watched her jump through the portal. Brant stood there for a moment watching the portal and the others standing on the beach as they looked back at Brant with a smile, and then he turned around and took a step toward Eclipse. No matter how it was going to end it would end today.

"**H**EY, ECLIPSE!" BRANT SHOUTED getting his attention. "If you want this, come and get it," he said tossing the orb in his hand.

"Ah!" Eclipse yelled in frustration throwing several black arrows all at once.

"Nope, nice try," Brant said ducking underneath. Brant got back to his feet as he started running toward Eclipse.

"Your arrogance will be your downfall," he replied. Suddenly, Eclipse waved his hand as hard as he could at the glass. The platform shattered as it fell apart making its way to Brant. He jumped over the glass wave as the platform shattered behind him, but there wasn't anything there for him to land on.

"Oh, no," Brant whispered to himself as he started to fall when he remembered what Selene said back at the valley. "Just think about what you want the light to do," he said to himself. He stretched his feet out and landed on a small yellow platform underneath his feet as yellow light showed from underneath his shoes. Eclipse's eyes got big as he watched Brant stand on air. "I don't feel like skydiving today, how about you?" Brant said with a smirk as he reached his hands down at the platform Eclipse was standing on and threw his arms to the side shattering the glass beneath his feet. Eclipse started to fall but as he fell, we waved his hands up and created a black stand. He landed on the platform he created and looked around at the glass falling. Eclipse grunted in frustration as he waved his hand upward as hard as he could making the platform fly up. Brant looked down as Eclipse swung a black hammer that formed in his hand as he swung. Eclipse hit Brant on the side of the head sending him flying back and dropping the Stabilizer in the process. Brant started to fall again but waved his hand upward creating another makeshift platform like Kit did. Brant landed on his back just as Eclipse caught the orb. Brant ran at Eclipse and jumped as hard as he could. He flew over Eclipse as Brant flipped on his head with his arm reached downward. Suddenly, the orb lit up yellow as it flew to Brant's hand. "I'll take that."

"Fool!" Eclipse said gritting his teeth. He threw his arm out creating a black pillar that latched onto Brant. Before Brant had a chance to respond as he hung upside down, Eclipse waved his hand up and slammed it down in the direction of the glass platform. The arm threw Brant up and back on the platform he recreated, landing hard as the light protected him as much as it could. He let go of the orb as it rolled to the edge of the platform as the pillar Eclipse stood on made its way toward the edge. He bent down and grabbed the orb as he stood on the glass platform as Brant still wasn't to his feet yet.

"Ow!" he said gritting his teeth as he stayed on his hands and knees. Eclipse looked down at Brant with a cold grin. He looked up at the portals that filled the sky with the citizens of the countless worlds watching.

"Behold!" Eclipse said addressing the spectators. "The one who was destined to defeat me. He was going to do what countless could not. This boy was going to do the one thing no one had done. He thought he could stand against the darkness," he said as Brant stood up watching Eclipse look at him with an arrogant smile. "The Renegade," he said with a grin. "Now, all of reality is mine," Eclipse said placing both hands on the Stabilizer. "But first," he said as he opened the orb. "Allow me to extinguish your light," Eclipse said when, suddenly, black sand surrounded Brant as it started to make his skin turn gray and crack.

"Ah!" Brant yelled in pain as he got on his hands and knees as the dark sand started to swallow him whole. He tried to run but couldn't move. He thought this was it as his skin turned more and more gray and cracked more and more when he heard a familiar voice in his head.

"Don't give up, Brant," he heard.

"What?" Brant asked, hearing a voice, but he didn't recognize it at first.

"You can do it Brant, fight," the voice said again but this time Brant recognized it.

"Mom?" Brant managed to get out as he looked up from the ground.

"You have everything you need to win," the voice said. Brant looked down at his hands and lit them up yellow making the darkness around his hands move back. Brant concentrated more as the darkness started to swallow him up. He took a deep breath as he closed his eyes. Suddenly, a bright light shone from his hands as the light started to make its way up Brant's arms. "Don't stop," the voice said as Brant slowly got up. Brant got to one foot as light shone out for a moment like his foot splashed in a puddle. Eclipse watched as the light started to shine brighter chasing away the darkness. Brant slowly stood up as the weight of the darkness started to get lighter and lighter. "Remember, I will always be proud of you," the voice finished. Brant smiled as his skin started to change back to normal and the light surrounded him. Brant straightened up with his eyes still closed focusing on the darkness as it vanished. Brant opened his eyes as he stood in the light. Eclipse took a step back in fear to see

Brant's eyes yellow as the light protected him in a way that was never done before.

"You're human, it's not possible," Eclipse said in fear. "How?" "You said it yourself," Brant started. "I'm The Renegade," he said standing tall. Eclipse started to raise his hands but Brant raised his hand first and a bright yellow beam shot at Eclipse. It struck Eclipse in the center of his chest as the continuous beam hit Eclipse. Brant watched as Eclipse's skin started to change from gray to a lighter shade of white as Eclipse tried to fight back.

"No!" He yelled in frustration being held back by the light. Eclipse looked up at Brant who still just stood in one place. "This madness will not stop with me," he started taking a deep breath. "There are some things far more frighting than dying, Renegade," Eclipse finished. Suddenly, he grabbed the blue orb inside the Reality Stabilizer making it explode and Eclipse with it as the platform shattered, stopping before it got to Brant. The light started to fade around Brant and his eyes faded back to normal. He looked up as the portals started to close gradually, and the clouds started to make their way to Brant. He took off running toward the portals as the glass platform started to deteriorate. Just as the clouds started to surround him, and the glass platform gave way, Brant jumped through the portal that led back home.

52

SELENE WATCHED AS THE pink-and-blue clouds flooded through the portal. They took a step back trying to get a good look if Brant jumped through but all they could see was the portal as it closed. They all watched as the portal shut. The beach stood in silence with some of the citizens of Reavella coming out to see what was happening. Selene looked through the clouds but couldn't see anything. She looked down at the ground as they all just watched where the portal stood wishing Brant was there when, suddenly, they heard a cough from inside the clouds. They looked up to see Brant walk through the wall of clouds as it started to fade away.

"Could've gone without all the special effects," Brant said with a cough. The crowd started to cheer as Selene walked over with everyone right behind her.

"That was impressive," she said with a grin.

"I know, that's why I came back just to hear you say that," Brant replied with a grin.

"Good thing I know you don't mean a word of it," Selene said with a smile as the others surrounded him.

"Selene," Kit said getting her attention. "Look," she said motioning to the city. They all looked up to see the people of Reavella cheering on the group of rebels.

"You did it, you freed Reavella!" Brant said looking at the group.

"We did it," Selene corrected. They smiled at each other, and then they looked back at the city as they cheered for them.

53

B RANT SAT ALONE ON top of a building overlooking Reavella. His legs dangled over the ledge with his phone in his hand and his EarPods in both ears. He looked down at his phone at the Voice Memo app and opened it where a list of recordings waited. Brant took a deep breath and opened the first of the recordings and his mother's voice came through.

"Dear Brant, I know these past few months have been hard on you, but I'm going to a better place," his mother started as Brant listened. *"I want you to know that everything will be okay, but promise me you'll never stop being you. There's a light inside you, unlike anything I've ever seen, and even though I'll never see what great things you will do, I know you will show the world the light that's in you and, once you find a group that loves you as much as I do, you'll be unstoppable. You are the light of my life, my little guppy that swims against the stream. My little Renegade,"* she said. Brant turned off the phone taking a deep breath trying to keep himself together. He looked up at the city as a tear slowly made its way down his cheek. He took another deep breath as he looked over the city as the sun bounced off the skyscrapers. Brant stood up and looked to his left where Selene was watching the city from the building next door. He jumped over the small gap between the structures and walked up next to Selene.

"You, okay?" Brant asked. She looked over at Brant with a smile and nodded.

"Yeah," she started. "This is the first time I've ever seen them free."

"Feels good," Brant said looking at the city.

"My father's rule finally came to an end," she added.

"Yeah, about that—" Brant started a little unsure not knowing how she'll take the news. "When Eclipse took me back to the palace, he looked in my mind to learn how to unlock the Stabilizer. I fought back as best I could, and somehow, I looked in his," he explained.

"You resisted my father?" Selene questioned impressed.

"Yeah," Brant answered as he continued. "But what if I told you, you weren't his daughter?" He asked.

"What?" Selene questioned back.

"Eclipse found you in an escape pod floating in space," Brant started. "I don't know where you were from. The escape pod had a navigation system but it was wiped clean when it was launched. However, there were three other pods that were logged with yours. There weren't any names attached, but it looks like you have two sisters and a brother," Brant explained. Selene looked down at the ground trying to process everything. "If you survived, they had too as well."

"I'm not the daughter of Eclipse," Selene said looking at the roof of the building they were on.

"Sorry, I had to be the one to tell you I—" Brant started when Selene hugged him.

"Thank you," she said grabbing Brant. Brant smiled and hugged her back as they stood there for a moment or two.

"Now all we have to do is find your sisters and brother," Brant said as they let go of each other.

"How hard can that be?" Alpha asked as they walked up to the two.

"Like a needle in a haystack," Brant joked.

"A what?" Solar questioned.

"Never mind," Brant answered with a chuckle.

"Selene," Kit interjected with a flat communicator in her hand. "Crystal said if we don't show up for the ceremony in the next five minutes, she'll make us outlaws again," Kit explained with a grin.

"They gave her way too much power when they assigned her as head of the council," Alpha said with a grin.

"We don't trust anyone better to rule Reavella until the council finds a suitable ruler," Solar interjected.

"True," Alpha agreed. "But if she lets that go to her head, we'll be stuck freeing this place again."

"I don't think you have to worry about that," Selene said with a smile. "But we better get going, though."

"After you," Brant said looking at Selene.

54

"RACE YOU," ALPHA SAID looking at his sister.

"Okay, on your mark, get set, go!" Kit said casually and took off running catching Alpha off guard.

"That was cold," Alpha said, taking off running with Solar right behind him. Brant smiled as they jumped over the edge of the building and jumped on the air. Brant took off one of his earbuds and handed it to Selene. She smiled, took the EarPod, and placed it in her ear just as *Dreaming* by Apollo LTD started to play.

"This is Reavella. They tell me the sun shines for eight months and rains the other four," he thought to himself as he jumped over the ledge of the building and ran on air following the others. "It may have a few scratches and dents but it's home; it's our home. Those who will attack us are relentless and crazy, but those who will stop them? Oh, even more so," Brant thought as Selene jumped over his head as they made their way to the palace. "We are the voice of light, and bit by bit we will change reality," he thought as they started to make their way down. "Oh, sure, we've been outcasted by society. We've been told we'll never amount to anything but we never let that stop us," Brant thought as a black stage came into view just in front of the palace. "Sure, our enemies will have armies, and they'll outnumber us a hundred to one, but our light is far stronger than anything they could throw at us, and trust me that light is inside you. If you didn't know that before. Well, I hope you do now. And we'll wear the name they've given us proudly. The ones who never stayed down, and the ones who flow against the stream. Who are we?" He thought as they all landed on the black stage "The Renegade!" Brant shouted just as the red ring around the palace changed from red to yellow and the crowd cheered as they stood looking out over the free people of Reavella.

55

"**T**OOK YOU LONG ENOUGH," a human girl with short green hair said as another figure walked into a slick black room wearing a black-and-purple outfit, but standing next to her was another teenage girl with bright white skin and brown eyes wearing a dark blue outfit, with long black hair, and holding a tablet with shackles around her wrist.

"I was gone for an hour, what happened?" The stranger asked.

"I know what it looks like but—" she answered as screens turned on showing images of Selene, Alpha, Kit, and Solar in Reavella just after Eclipse was defeated. "Reality didn't collapse, but it was on the brink of it," she explained.

"Who did this?" The stranger asked.

"This guy," the girl answered just as an image of Brant fighting Eclipse came up. "They call him *The Renegade*," she said as the stranger looked down at the image.

"He's more than that," he replied.

"How do you know that?" The girl asked. The stranger just looked down at the image of Brant and smiled as the light of the screen bounced off his face.

Want to dive deeper into the story? Well, here's the *music* featured, and even got an honorable mention in *The Renegade*.

Brant's Reality Mix
—*Letters to the President*, Hawk Nelson
—*Meant to Live*, Switchfoot
—*Mercy's Shore*, NEEDTOBREATHE
—*Billboards on Sunset*, Sarah Reeves
—*The Prodigal*, Josiah Queen
—*Tonight*, FM Static
—*Whatever It Takes*, Stephen Stanley
—*Dreaming*, Apollo LTD